SWEARING

OFF

STARS

SWEARING
OFF
STARS

A Novel

by

DANIELLE M. WONG

SHE WRITES PRESS

Published 2017
Printed in the United States of America
ISBN: 978-1-63152-284-0 pbk
ISBN: 978-1-63152-285-7 ebk
Library of Congress Control Number: 2017944428

Book design by Stacey Aaronson

For information, address:
She Writes Press
1563 Solano Ave #546
Berkeley, CA 94707

She Writes Press is a division of SparkPoint Studio, LLC.

For my father, Derrick Wong.
I miss you in the light, dark, and everywhere between.

PART I

Prologue

Wonderland, January 1920

It's a dark, starless night in the woods, and part of me wants to turn around. There's so much energy inside my head—transitory thoughts and heavy regrets. The ache worsens as I make my way through the towering redwoods. I want to take it all back, the detrimental words and their cruel repercussions. But I can't . . . and I can't turn back now.

I strike the match before tossing it far in front of me, a split second of doubt and nothing more. With the simple flick of my wrist, one tiny golden spark transforms before my eyes. Beautifully ominous flames abound in seconds. Even if I wanted to take this back, it would be far too late. The grounds are already brilliantly ablaze with inferno and chaos.

I walk quickly as my paranoia proliferates into a beast of its own. I'm jogging now, treading on the shrubbery I've passed a thousand times or more. It's so dark that I can't see my own fingertips, much less what's in front of me. But it doesn't matter. I know every fraction of this forest—every branch of every tree.

I'm far away from the fire now, but its blaring roar convinces me otherwise. I stop running and feel the sharp air mount in my chest, a piercing pain exacerbated by the cold. The sting makes my eyes water as I attempt to catch my breath. Moments later, I turn around to face the amber glow.

I feel numb as I stare into the flames before me. *She's gone. Because of me.* Bittersweet memories of our time together flood my mind until the fire has wholly consumed the building in its wake. *We ended because of me.*

And just like that, Wonderland is no more.

Chapter 1

Oxford, August 1919

LIA

Cases of unopened rouge and globs of melted lipstick lined my cluttered vanity. I sighed as I looked into the smudgy mirror hanging from my ecru bedroom walls. The beauty class my mother had so fervently encouraged me to take the previous summer had yet to pay off. A halfhearted swipe of mascara was all I could handle.

I ironed a navy dress and finger-combed my chestnut mane into a disordered braid. My boyish frame looked particularly plain that morning, accented by the dress's straight cut. Typical back-to-school fears buzzed through my head—*getting lost, not knowing anyone, and being the strange new girl.* All legitimate, might I add.

The main campus was a brisk ten-minute walk from my front door. Well, not *my* door, per se. I was staying with the Watson family in their large Victorian home. My father had never met Mr. Watson personally, but they shared a mutual friend named Teddy Graves. I didn't quite understand the connection, and my father never explained how they knew each other.

All I *did* know was that after the war ended, my father told Teddy about my desire to travel—something that transpired after a few too many drinks, since my dad would have never done that while sober. Teddy mentioned my wish to Mr. Watson, who then offered to let me live with his family in England for the year. Mrs. Watson even wrote me a kind letter and insisted that I stay for as long as I wished. I intended to take full advantage of her offer, especially since I was away from home for the first time in my life.

The Watsons lived in a well-to-do neighborhood called Spindly Oaks. It was the kind of place that made you wonder if any of the residents were as interesting as their grand mansions and beautiful yards. Everyone I'd seen thus far looked like they'd stepped out of a department store window or holiday catalog, groomed and primped to perfection.

Luckily for me, the walk from Spindly Oaks to my destination was a beautiful one. I've always loved being outdoors, so I couldn't wait to explore the surrounding area and campus grounds. Grand oaks towered over late summery blossoms as tiny birds sang sweet songs. The scent of fresh pine flooded my nostrils as I left the Watsons' protected neighborhood behind. I couldn't believe I was finally there. I was about to study at my dream school, the University of Oxford.

I'd made sure to cover all my bases. I'd purchased course books ahead of time, borrowed a souvenir campus map from a friend back home, and was now leaving for class two hours early, just in case. Unfortunately, my tattered map was a bit inconsistent. Somerville College was nowhere to be found. My remaining sense of calm quickly evaporated.

When I finally arrived at the correct building, a flyer notified me that my first class had been canceled due to a shortage of enrolled students and would be moved to the following semester. The university housed hundreds of soldiers during the war, and students were still trickling back in slowly. Wartime only ended the year before I arrived, so Oxford's campus was still sprawling with leftover soldiers. This lack of students meant that I would be taking economics instead, a subject I hadn't prepared for whatsoever.

Overwhelmed and confused, I raced to the library to try to track down the books I needed for this new course. As I ran, an unexpected August wind flushed my fair cheeks and rustled my thick hair. My braid quickly became a sad excuse for an attempted hairstyle.

I quickly turned a corner to escape the cruel wind and collect my thoughts—and as I did, my hand-me-down book bag slipped off my shoulder and sent my textbooks crashing onto the cold pavement beneath my feet.

I collapsed and buried my face into my shaky hands. Tears welled in my eyes, and I tried to blink them away. All of my worries were coming to a head: I wasn't cut out for Oxford.

Right then, a group of chic British students walked toward me. I was more embarrassed than I had been in a while. There I was, sitting on the ground with my used books scattered around me and cheap makeup running down my face, and now I had an audience.

"Oh dear," a sweet voice whispered.

A pair of pointed black flats stood square in front of me. I slowly looked up and met their owner's eyes—emerald gems that would catch anyone off guard. She knelt down and motioned for the rest of her group to continue on.

"I'll catch up with you later!" she called after them.

A flurry of two-toned shoes disappeared into the distance.

"First day?" she asked coyly.

I nodded and wiped my eyes. "Is it that obvious?"

"You're American," she said with a smile. Her perfect pink lips revealed a straight set of pearly teeth. "*Scarlett*," she said, extending a polished hand.

I shook it and felt the coolness of her stacked silver rings as they pressed gently into my palm.

"Lia," I said quietly. "Lia Cole."

"Short for Amelia?" she asked, brushing a lock of blond hair over her slim shoulders.

I nodded again. She was the first person I had actually enjoyed talking to since arriving in England. My few conversations with the Watsons felt stiff and forced.

"Why are you crying, Amelia? It's only day one."

I just stared at her. Scarlett's voice sounded like an eloquent stage actress's, elevated with a posh British accent.

"Here," she said and knelt down beside me. She took my hair in her hands and rebraided it slowly. Every gentle tug put me further at ease, like everything was being woven back into order. I got lost in the floral scent wafting from behind me, and I wondered which expensive perfume Scarlett was wearing. Then she pulled a coral ribbon out of her bag and tied it around the end of my now-perfect braid.

"Thank you," I whispered as I turned around to face her.

She gave me the slightest nod and another demure smile. I noticed a beautiful silver cuff sparkling on her slender wrist, but before I could say anything, she quickly adjusted it and stood up.

"You'll be all right, Amelia." Scarlett winked and brushed off her ruby drop-waist dress. Then, with a swift flutter of heavy lashes, she was gone.

I watched in awe as her petite hourglass frame moved further and further away. After she faded from view I sat on the ground for a while longer, thinking about the girl I'd just met. I wanted to know more about her. I didn't even know Scarlett's last name, but I had a comforting and hopeful feeling that we'd become friends. I warmed at the thought.

Then I noticed students pointing at me like a museum display, and my surroundings came back into focus. I stood up and resumed my route to the library.

FIVE mind-numbing hours later, I was back at the Watson residence, inhaling the smell of hearty beef stew that lingered in their entryway. I slipped out of my tight Mary Janes, and my feet relaxed instantly. More mouthwatering aromas drifted in from the remodeled kitchen; I tiptoed over and saw Mrs. Watson standing near the stove. A tray of piping hot butter rolls caught my eye before I noticed the heaping pot of simmering stew.

"Oh, hello dear. How was class?"

Of course I told her it was wonderful before heading upstairs to my room. But the truth was, my classes had been nothing exciting. I didn't really know what to say about them. I'd done well in school my entire life, turning in decent work and earning good marks. But it felt like I was just going through the motions most of the time. Despite my best efforts to take interest in each subject, I was anything but fully engaged.

I'd never revealed this to either of my parents. After all, I was still in shock that they'd let me come to England in the first place. Home was so far away—another country entirely, with an ocean between. I finally felt like their enduring hold over me had loosened. If I was a bird, my cage door was opening. And I wanted nothing more than to fly away.

It wasn't that I didn't love or care for my parents. On the contrary, I respected them with every fiber of my being. My mother was a brilliant Italian woman, and my father a German immigrant, though his Brooklyn accent had since dominated his former one. They had fallen in love and built a life together from the ground up. I had witnessed their struggles firsthand and had a strong appreciation for the sacrifices they'd made for our family.

We owned a restaurant in Brooklyn called Selena's, named after my mom's grandmother. Mom and Dad created a unique menu of German meets Italian: herbed steak with sauerkraut and roasted vegetables, spiced Bavarian sausages over linguini, handmade raviolis with sage butter and broccoli. It had taken a while before we turned a profit, but the restaurant had since become a neighborhood staple.

Aside from being hard workers, my parents were also the most protective people I knew. Mom said it was their way of loving me, but it bordered on smothering—made worse by the fact that I had no siblings to share the burden with. This protectiveness increased during the war, understandably so. For a while, I spent as much time away from home as possible, to the point that both of my parents took notice and began threatening to move us to another state. I never understood how that would have solved anything, but I also believed that it was an empty threat. There was no way they'd leave their precious restaurant behind.

Back when my summer plans consisted solely of working at Selena's, I started looking for other options. That was when they introduced me to Robbie Wells.

"Dinner!"

Mrs. Watson's shrill voice halted my train of thought. I walked downstairs to the gaudy dining room, preparing myself to make obligatory conversation with the Watsons for the next hour or so.

That night, Mr. Watson told me all about his successful day at the bank and how he "showed those pissers what real money was." I nodded politely in between oversized bites of beef stew while Mrs. Watson egged him on—"Oh Brucey, you're amazing, darling!"

Needless to say, I had to work hard to keep my dinner down. Mr. and Mrs. Watson reminded me of everything I never wanted to be—one of those wealthy couples who threw outlandish parties but didn't really have any true friends. Mrs. Watson was okay by herself, but she turned into a different person around him. It was like she was playing a part: the doting housewife to his arrogant breadwinner. I cringed at the idea of ever marrying someone like that.

"Jesus, girl. Are you even listening?"

Mr. Watson was staring at me through drunken eyes. I looked around the table, unsure of what to say.

Mrs. Watson cleared her throat politely. "Brucey, darling, don't you think you've had enough for tonight?" She gestured to his empty scotch glass.

He cocked his head and glared at her menacingly.

"I'll get you another glass, then," she said feebly. "Lia, perhaps you should go upstairs and finish your homework."

I hesitantly stood up and cleared my plate. Their boys, Christian and Thomas, were playing with their food and seemed oblivious to the tension in the room. Mrs. Watson nodded and muttered something under her breath.

LATER that night, I couldn't stop thinking about Scarlett. I pulled the coral ribbon out of my hair and turned it over in my fingers. I didn't even understand what I was feeling. I pictured her outfit, perfectly tailored and polished. Her manicured nails, a ruby red to match the modern dress she was wearing. Her fashionable book bag, made of brown leather and filled with who-knows-what?

She was gorgeous, obviously. Scarlett looked like the lead actress in a big-time picture, with an arresting smile and bright eyes to boot. But it was something *more*—perhaps her inimitable attitude. I'd spoken with her for all of five minutes, but already knew that she was incomparable. Scarlett was mesmerizing: she was the person schoolgirls imitated—the woman men fought for.

I shook my head and opened my copy of *First Year Economics.* I needed to focus and get her out of my mind. What was wrong with me? I'd only ever obsessed this much over boys. Well, one in particular . . .

Robbie was a bank teller in the city. We'd gone to school in bordering neighborhoods, but had never met until his family supplied furniture to our restaurant. My parents instantly connected with them, so, naturally, I was encouraged to connect with their son as well.

I hated the situation at first. It felt like an arrangement between our bloodlines, merely a suitable match. But something changed the summer after we met. Robbie was kind, polite, and sweet. He took me to the movies and out to fancy dinners—until I told him that I hated expensive meals, at which point he laughed and suggested a little diner downtown. That was what I loved about him. He *listened.* Besides my grade school friends, he was the only person who actually cared about what I had to say.

The pages of *First Year Economics* fell into my lap as I drifted into a light sleep.

"Found a good one," he calls out from across the field.

I run quickly through rows of sweet apple trees to find him.

"Robbie!" I'm laughing and running, inhaling whiffs of ripe fruit as I go. Suddenly I see him, standing next to the wooden ladder he made for apple picking.

"There you are." He smiles as he pulls me into his arms. He feels so good.

"I found you," I whisper.

He nuzzles my nose and kisses me tenderly. "You found me," he whispers back.

I was jolted awake by my clanging alarm clock. It made the most obnoxious sound that startled me every day, without fail. I turned it off and rolled over underneath my fort of covers. I would stay in bed until the last possible moment, even if it meant forgoing my usual half-hearted attempt at makeup application.

I climbed out of my four-poster bed and pulled back the blue linen curtains framing my oval window. The early-morning darkness stared back at me, daring me to go home. I quietly refused and resolved to *give it another go*, as the Brits say.

Soon I was out the door and on my way to day number two of classes. The crisp air rustled my campus map as I navigated my way to mathematics class. I had purchased an updated version from the student store the previous day, hoping desperately that it wouldn't lead me astray, and my eyes were now glued to the thin charcoal line I'd drawn when mapping out my route the night before.

"Miss! Hello?"

I barely heard the female voice before I bumped into its owner.

"Oh, I'm sorry!" I said as I looked up into a pair of pale blue eyes.

The girl appeared to be about my age, maybe a couple years older. "Don't worry about it," she said, laughing. "Looks like you're trying to find something important?"

"Yes, my mathematics course. Lady Margaret Hall?"

"I can take you there if you like," she replied cheerfully.

"Okay, sure," I said, a little wary. I couldn't help but feel like she had some sort of ulterior motive.

"I'm Ida." She smiled and extended a hand. Her curly black hair was pulled back, emphasizing her swan-like neck and lengthy physique.

"Lia, short for Amelia."

"Nice to meet you, Lia. So are you new here? A freshie, I mean."

"Yes." I smiled back, thinking I really needed to work on an incognito approach to map reading.

"What are you studying?"

"Liberal Arts," I answered. "But I'm only here for the academic year."

"Same here. Regarding the major, not the length of study at Oxford," she clarified. "It's one of the few majors afforded to us female students." There was an air of bitterness in her tone.

"Mmmm . . ." I really couldn't think of a decent response.

"You *do* realize that as women, we aren't allowed to matriculate with the male students." The sentence hung there, something between a statement and a question.

"I—I didn't know that."

"Yes, it's an awful rule. I'm surprised that you hadn't heard . . ." There was an odd levity in her voice that starkly contrasted with our conversation topic.

"Well, like I said . . . I'm new here."

"It upsets many of us," Ida continued as she tugged on the hem of her lilac dress. "Not just the ladies, but some of the men too."

"Oh?"

I honestly wasn't that interested. I would be graduating from a university back in the States, whether I wanted to or not.

"Yes, Lia. It's a big deal in the grand scheme of things. Most men think that we're lucky to even be here at all."

She shuffled through her black book bag. "Please at least take a flyer."

"Of course," I said, reading the thick pink paper:

WOMEN'S RIGHT TO MATRICULATE AT OXFORD
Align with the movement and fight for equality!

"Our meetings take place in a secret location so they can't shut us down," she said proudly.

"So who can't shut you down?"

Ida looked at me as if I had just asked the daftest question. "*Them.*" She gestured toward a black police car pulling up the drive.

As the car drew closer, the rolled-down window revealed two angry men in uniform.

"You lot! Not this again! Get a move on, will ya?"

I turned back to face Ida, but she was long gone, leaving only a trail of pink paper in her wake.

No sooner had I leaned down to pick up my book bag than a large hand grabbed my shoulder. I whipped around as quickly as Ida had run away. The officer looked surprised.

"Eh, I've never seen you before. We've got a new girl, Jim!"

"I—I'm a new student," I stuttered. "Sir."

"Then what are you doing hanging around with this crowd?"

He waved a pink flyer in front of my stunned face.

"Really, I was just on my way to class—"

"Tell you what. Don't get mixed up with these blighters anymore. You hear me?"

His tone was less threatening than before, but all I could do was nod my head.

"Go on!" He gestured toward the campus buildings, pointing a plump finger at the path Ida had taken. I hurried off before he could say another word. Although I did catch the last thing he muttered under his coffee-scented breath: "Crazy girls. When will they give it up, Jim?"

I hadn't even noticed the sun come up during that confusing series of events. Still shaken from the proceedings, I sat through three classes uninterested and finished out my week in a similar manner. I managed to arrive on time each day, though after that day I chose to ask for directions instead of using my map. It had already gotten me into trouble once now, and I wasn't interested in running into any more students with agendas and pink flyers.

Chapter 2

As a new month began, I vowed to spend more time around campus and less time stuck inside with the Watsons. Although I was grateful for their hospitality, one could only tolerate so much conversation with Mr. Watson. He drank too much almost every night, which turned him into an even angrier narcissist than he already was. I even heard him telling Mrs. Watson one night that I should be more appreciative and start helping their maids clean the house. She protested at first, but quickly gave in when his tone reached a threatening pitch.

I'd never seen the maids around the house, but figured that they cleaned while I was in class—the house was always in good order, and I was under the impression that they were more than capable. But apparently I was mistaken, since from then on I got assigned *domestic chores* any time I wasn't doing homework or reading in my room.

I started to take more notice of the couple's weekday behavior. Mrs. Watson woke up early and put on a full face of makeup before creeping downstairs to brew coffee. Mr. Watson's alarm rang at exactly seven each morning. His bedroom door creaked open about an hour later, and he emerged showered, shampooed, and shaven.

Unlike Mrs. Watson's soft footsteps, Mr. Watson's stride had a way of shaking the entire house. This naturally caused the children to jump out of bed and run downstairs after their father, which meant they all arrived in the kitchen at approximately the same time—and Mrs. Watson was always ready for them with a freshly cooked breakfast.

I heard and smelled all of the morning commotion from my corner bedroom on the second story. Sometimes when I didn't have class, I'd just wake up and lie there, listening to them start their days. Only after the family's driver, Vincent, picked up Thomas and Christian for school would I ease my way into the kitchen and brew another pot of coffee.

I'd sit at the table and say good morning to Mrs. Watson, who was usually dressed in an expensive floral number that belonged on a store mannequin. She would pause only briefly to say hello, then immediately resume her erratic house-cleaning routine, shuffling around the lower level, dusting fine china, and attending to the occasional fern. I began to wonder where the maids that Mr. Watson had drunkenly boasted about weeks earlier were.

One morning I found a handwritten list on the kitchen counter. It was damp and laid underneath Mr. Watson's pricey cigarettes. The note read, *Chores for Lia and maids: wash dishes in sink, sweep living room, etc.* I rolled my eyes and walked over to the sink. There wasn't a dish in sight. I turned around to see Mrs. Watson carrying a broom into the other room. As I opened my mouth to say something, she winked and began to sweep the shiny hardwood floor.

I realized that I had two hours before my final class on Wednesday, perfect for a late lunch break. There weren't as many students roaming around the campus as earlier, so I walked up to a woman in a black beret to ask where the cafeteria was.

"Excuse me, I was wondering if—"

She turned around before I could finish my question.

"Oh, I didn't realize it was you," I said, shocked.

"It's the beret," Scarlett whispered with a playful smile. She held her finger up to her lips, like she was hiding from something.

"It is." I smiled back, wondering how she managed to fit all of those blonde locks into such a tiny hat.

"Where are you headed, Amelia?"

"Oh, it's just Lia," I corrected her. "And I'm off for lunch."

"Amelia suits you better," she teased. "I was going to eat something too. Do you want to join?"

"Sounds good. Where to?"

"Just follow me," she said with the quick flick of a red nail.

We walked in silence for what felt like ages. The clusters of buildings had evolved into trees and hilly gardens.

"Um, Scarlett, aren't we going a little far?"

The truth was that my new boots were killing me. We were treading through some sort of off-campus forest.

"Tired already, Amelia?" she teased.

"No, it's just . . ." She was right. I was winded after a mere cross-campus walk. "Never mind."

"Ah, that's the spirit," she winked at me. "Don't worry, love. This place is worth it."

A sudden breeze blew open the flap of my bag, exposing the pink flyer Ida had so kindly left me with the week before. Scarlett noticed it before I could close the flap.

"The women's movement. Are you a supporter?" She raised a steady blond eyebrow in my direction.

"That depends," I ventured. "Are you?"

She looked at me in surprise for a moment. "Of course," she said firmly, adjusting her silver bracelet. "Now your turn. Are *you?*"

"I'm not sure yet." The words came out before I could craft a proper response.

"I see." Scarlett stopped dead in her tracks. I wondered if she was going to leave me for dead just because I didn't support the cause.

"It's . . . I've only just heard about it. I need to learn more, I think." That was the simple truth.

"Fair enough, Amelia. We'll just have to give you an education."

Scarlett put her arm around my shoulder and led me closer to the lodge-like building in front of us. I was so distracted that I hadn't noticed it, or the sign next to it that read *Wonderland*.

She quickly ushered me under two ivy arches and through a rosebud-covered courtyard. Suddenly we weren't at a University but wandering through some sort of secret fairyland in the middle of the woods.

"Well, look who it is," echoed a lively voice from across the courtyard.

"Shhh," Scarlett said coyly. "We're trying to make a grand entrance."

A tall figure walked toward us, a man's body with boyish features. His dimples grew more defined as he approached. He slid his hand around Scarlett's tiny waist and planted a soft kiss on her pink lips. I felt simultaneous pangs of protectiveness and curiosity.

"No one's here at the moment," he told her.

"Darn." She sighed. "I wanted to introduce her to everyone!" Then she turned to face me.

"Amelia Cole, meet William Masterson."

"Pleasure," I said with a nod.

"Just Will," he said and shook my hand with a quick wink.

"And I'm just Lia," I said, smiling. "But she won't call me anything other than my full name."

"She's oddly formal like that." He laughed and scooped Scarlett into his arms. "C'mon, *just* Lia. Follow us!"

We walked into a cream-colored building with a wooden door that didn't look tall enough to fit someone of Will's stature. Even Scarlett had to hunch just to make it through the entrance.

"You'll get used to it, don't worry." She must have noticed my confused expression.

"What is this place?" I wondered out loud.

We were making our way down a spiral staircase, which explained the shockingly low entrance. A musty scent emanated from below. We were getting farther and farther underground. Glowing lanterns illuminated an otherwise dim hallway at the bottom of the staircase. They cast a warm, amber light on several floor vases lining the hall—bright poppies and lavender bunches peeked out of terracotta cylinders and emerald glasses.

"This," Scarlett whispered, "is *Wonderland*."

We approached a large room at the end of the mysterious hallway. It smelled of lavender oil and cigarette smoke—an odd combination that caught me off guard. I stared up at the room's high ceilings and noticed a tiny rectangular window. It provided a refreshing light source in the otherwise shadowy room— thick vines and rich green ivy crawled through its opening and reminded me of Scarlett's eye color.

The rest of the room was filled with red leather armchairs spread out around a thick wooden table. Stacks of paper covered its surface; file folders occupied the tall bookshelves leaning against a set of yellowing walls. I recognized the pink papers as the protest flyers Ida had been passing out. As if realizing this, Scarlett broke the silence.

"Welcome to our headquarters, Amelia."

I looked up in disbelief.

"You're . . ."

"Yes."

"But . . ."

"What, I don't seem like the protesting type?"

I blinked twice, trying to take it all in. "I'm not really sure what I'm doing here," I said, suddenly wanting to leave.

"You didn't already tell her?" Will sounded surprised.

"Tell me what?"

"We want to recruit you. For our movement."

"If this is about the women's rights issue, I already explained to Ida that I'm not even going to be here next year . . ."

"Christ, Ida . . ." Scarlett trailed off, rubbing her temples. "Look, we've known that there was going to be an American student here for a while now. And to be honest, the team thinks that it would really help our cause. You know, to have some different voices involved."

"So you've been waiting to snatch me up?" I was suddenly confused—disappointed, even.

"I won't lie to you, Amelia," Scarlett said. "I sort of sought you out the other day. I mean, I wasn't expecting to find you in such a . . . vulnerable state, but—"

"Well, I don't want any part in this. I'm just here to study and experience a new country for a few months. That's it."

"Will you please just listen to what we have to say?" Will pleaded. "It'll only take a couple moments."

I stood there staring at them, withholding my response just for the sake of it.

"Fine," I finally said. "Just for a few moments."

They told me all about their mission. The team wanted equality for male and female students. There were important disparities that I hadn't even realized existed. Women couldn't truly matriculate at Oxford, regardless of their academic performance. We were allowed to attend lectures, enroll in classes, and even take exams. But none of that really mattered, did it? We couldn't earn an actual degree.

Scarlett, Will, and their friends had come together to try to change this. They were doing everything in their power to transform the system. I was skeptical at first, but listened intently as Scarlett told me about women's suffrage in England. The war started a political movement that resulted in certain women being allowed to vote—*some, but not all*. Scarlett and Will realized that parliament still had a long way to go, but that they could start small. If they achieved their goal at Oxford, women would be able to graduate from the university alongside men.

It didn't take much more to get me interested. My stubborn resistance quickly dissolved as I heard Scarlett and Will speak about their cause with such passion. They believed in academic equality and were fighting for it. I longed to be part of something so genuine.

We spent the remainder of that day discussing plans and backup plans. I was shocked at how intrigued I became in such a short time. They were both so brilliant, so well-spoken. I wanted to be like that. I wanted a reason to be like that. As the afternoon sun set into a dusty pink sky, I realized that I had skipped my late class without a second thought. My long walk back to the Watsons' took me through a winding patch of oak trees. They reminded me of the ones from home—dark and solid in their depth. My mind wandered as I remembered scaling the tree near Robbie's house. We were probably too old to climb trees, but we did it anyway.

"Grab that branch to the right," Robbie suggests as he lifts me up.

I reach for the thick brown branch and come up short.

"You're getting heavy, Cole," he jokes.

"Oh shut up," I laugh as I try to reach higher.

"Have you been eating too much of your mother's pasta?" he continues to prod.

"Got it!" I yell victoriously as I pull myself up the to the next branch. I keep climbing until Robbie looks unsettlingly tiny.

"Hello up there," he calls.

I laugh and delight in my tree-climbing success.

"You're almost to the top. Just go for it!"

I glance up nervously and see the highest point of the tree I'm wrapped around.

"C'mon Cole!"

I swallow hard and dig my shoes into the ridged trunk. After I reach the top, I manage to get myself onto a branch thick enough to support me. I sit on it nervously, scratched legs dangling as Robbie cheers from below.

Just then, I see two uniformed figures approaching the house behind my best friend. I convince myself that they're salesmen, but I know that they're probably soldiers. I point cautiously while my other hand grips the trunk tightly. Robbie turns around as they knock on the door. I watch it open slowly, Mrs. Wells standing in the arched doorway. One of the soldiers shakes his head and says something inaudible. Robbie runs toward the house as his mother drops to her knees.

※

THE next week passed quickly as I tried to balance my academics with these new meetings and rallies. Scarlett and I ate lunch together regularly. The more I got to know her, the more attractive and mysterious she became. A dichotomy of sorts: classy and sophisticated, but surprisingly unpretentious. Serious, but mind-numbingly funny when she wanted to be.

"Everyone will be there today," she told me as we paced through the woods one day.

"I'll be happy to meet them. So far I only know you and Will," I realized out loud.

"You'll love them," she assured me.

I hoped she was right. As we approached the magical lodge known as *Wonderland*, I paused to find my compact.

"Oh, we haven't got time for that now!"

"I just want to look presentable . . ."

"You always look great, Amelia. *Really*."

"Always?" I said. "If you think back to a couple weeks ago, I didn't make the greatest first impression on you . . . salty tears and mascara running down my cheeks sound familiar?"

She stopped walking. "That's when I knew you were perfect."

"What are you talking about?" I searched her face for something I didn't yet realize I was looking for.

"For the team, I mean. The movement. You were so helpless that day, but you also possessed this quiet strength . . . It's fascinating, really. I knew we could put it to good use." She shrugged.

"Scar—"

"Amelia. We don't have time to stand around and talk all day, you know. We should go inside."

There it was. A moment of vulnerability, cut off by Scarlett's sense of urgency.

"Okay," I sighed. And once again, I followed her inside.

She was right about everything. I loved the other members and their different points of view. There were men and women of different ages, all united by their desire for this change. With each person I spoke to, I felt more connected to the group as a whole.

There was Thomas, whose mother was one of the first women to ever study at Oxford; Mary, a chemistry student who wanted a fair shot at working alongside the men she was taking exams with. In her words, *Why shouldn't everyone be fighting for this?* And then there was David, a fellow freshman who had initially been taken in by the revolutionary appeal when he and Will, who was his roommate, got to talking about the movement one night over beers. The rest was history. David reminded me of Robbie—they were both well-spoken and had each lost a brother in the war.

I left that meeting with a greater sense of what we were really doing. After all, there was a stark difference between a roomful of kids talking about revolution and a group actually committed to taking the (sometimes small) steps necessary to enact change. As I drifted off to sleep that night, fantasies of earning a diploma at the school crept into my subconscious. All I could dream about was how gratifying it would be to have my name announced at Oxford's 1922 graduation ceremony.

Chapter 3

SCARLETT

The only thing more disconcerting than losing your head is losing your coveted appointment. I'm already up to my ears in coursework and now *this*. Will tells me that the school board is pushing back our presentation *yet again*. Don't they possess even a thread of civility? This is the fifth time we've rescheduled the bloody thing.

We immediately call an emergency meeting and regroup. Ida volunteers to speak with the board one more time while Will and I draw up a new proposal submission. Then Freddie, who never says a bloody word at meetings, decides to speak up. At first I roll my eyes and mentally tune him out. But then he says something I'm not expecting.

See, Freddie is on the international student committee here at Oxford. He pulls out a file—Lord knows how he got a hold of it—and sets it on the table in front of me. I flip open the manila cover and pull out a profile sheet. *Amelia Cole, 18 years old, American*, etc. She looks nice enough and definitely has the right credentials, or lack thereof.

I pass the sheet around and give Freddie a quick nod of approval. Will grins when he reads it, looking at me with bright eyes. He's thinking exactly what I am. For whatever reason, the board tends to listen to foreign students more than Brits. With this Amelia girl, we'll be well on our way. It's downright brilliant.

And then I meet Amelia face-to-face. There's something different about her that I can't put my finger on. I'm not sure if it's good or bad—it's just different. When I see her blubbering on the ground, there are no words. She looks so forlorn . . . completely vulnerable. It tugs on my heart a little.

So I help Amelia gather her books and rebraid her mop of chestnut hair. I don't even mention the movement—it's not the right time. A few students stare obnoxiously, but I sit with her until she stops crying. It just feels like the right thing to do.

Chapter 4

LIA

I woke up early after a particularly restless night of sparse dreams. As I stared out into the darkness, I realized that I was the only one awake in the Watson household. Intrigued by the thought of sneaking downstairs, I crawled out of bed and slowly turned my door handle.

The entire hallway was dark as I began to descend the spiral staircase. The sleepy silence made it difficult to walk downstairs without making noise I felt sure would wake the boys, but I finally reached the lower landing and made my way into a cozy reading nook. Unlike the sterile living room, this part of the house wasn't completely devoid of charm and comfort. I plopped myself down on the inviting sofa and laid my head on a soft navy pillow.

Barely any time passed before I heard someone coming down the staircase I'd used just minutes earlier. I straightened up and quickly looked around the room. As I started to stand, Mrs. Watson appeared in the doorway with a tiny lantern. I fell back into my seat and tried to hide the shock from my face.

This was not the Mrs. Watson I'd come to expect. Her

usually coiffed hair was frizzy and unstyled, sticking out on both sides of her head. Her face was bare—seemed stark naked without the heavy foundation and lipstick she always wore. A robe and furry slippers replaced her typical floral dress and heels. Even in the soft lantern light, I saw a world of difference in her appearance.

Neither of us spoke for a while. The moment was unexpected and awkward, something I never thought would happen. Mrs. Watson was supposed to be the perfect British housewife, never caught without a chic outfit or flawless red lips.

I was even more confused when she rubbed her tired eyes and left the room. I wondered if I should go back upstairs and pretend that I never saw her in her pajamas. But moments later, she reemerged with two mugs of warm chamomile tea. She handed me one and sat down on the sofa.

"Can't sleep?" she finally asked.

"No," I whispered.

"Me neither," she agreed.

"Bad dreams?" I ventured.

She shook her head and took a long sip. "I never really dream anymore."

"Why?" I wondered aloud.

The thought of Mrs. Watson lying perfectly still in bed was actually quite easy to picture.

"In fact," she continued. "I don't really sleep, either."

I wasn't sure why she was telling me this. Our normal routine of respectful coexistence was working out just fine.

"I'm sure you've heard me waking up at the crack of dawn every day . . ."

"Well, yes." I smiled and stared into my tea mug. "You do so much during the day, I just—"

"Thought I wanted an early start?" She raised a sparse, unpenciled eyebrow.

I shrugged and took another sip of soothing chamomile.

"You can sleep down here if you want. I was just about to go back to bed—"

"Oh, no dear. I have to get ready and put on my face before Mr. Watson wakes up. God, if he saw me like this . . ." She turned away.

I suddenly felt bad for her. The way she hid beneath an armor of product and formula, a shield of expensive material and printed roses.

"I think you look fine," I said.

She finger-combed her hair before turning back around. "You're sweet for saying so." She forced a smile.

I struggled to find a decent response.

"So . . . how did you and Mr. Watson meet?" I hoped that a change of subject would help.

The long pause that followed my question had me worried, but then her eyes lit up. "I was a shop girl in London. Bruce worked at a department store across the street. He came in every now and then to visit with our manager, Charles." Mrs. Watson set her mug on the floor.

"So Bruce started talking to me one day during my break. I was a shy girl, but he made me laugh and smile all the time. He'd bring wildflowers and walk me home after work. He was the sweetest young man I'd ever met."

I tried not to reveal my growing disbelief.

"We would dress up and go out dancing with our friends . . ."

Mrs. Watson began tracing the outline of her lips, almost like she was applying invisible rouge. Her face fell as the memory faded. "He doesn't always warm up to other people these days. I'm sure you've noticed . . ." She trailed off.

"I don't want to overstay my welcome," I said. "I've seen the lists written for me; the chores and—"

"Oh, don't bother with those. Bruce needs his little hierarchy of order."

"It's just—"

"You're wondering why I finish them myself?"

I nodded.

"Gives me something to do." She sighed. "Bruce doesn't want me working. You know how men are . . ."

She stared at the blank wall in front of us.

"What about the maids?"

"No maids," she said quickly. "I let them all go. Frankly, we don't need the help."

My confused expression made her laugh.

"It's just easier if I take care of it myself. I don't want any more *incidents.*"

I raised an eyebrow at her.

"Well." She hesitated. "Mr. Watson came home one day to find his polo trophy sitting on the mantelpiece, covered in dust. One of the maids had missed it by mistake and—"

She threw a bony hand into the air, as if to swat away the rest of the sentence. I stared at her as she fidgeted nervously on the sofa.

"He drinks after work, you see . . ."

I nodded slightly.

"The alcohol . . . it doesn't agree with him anymore," she said, staring into her lap. "Scotch and whiskey sort of turn him into a different person—"

Her voice broke, and I suddenly understood Mr. Watson's offensiveness.

"It's a bizarre life," she ruminated. "You grow up careless and free, thinking that the world is a beautiful place."

"Isn't it?"

"Not for everyone." She shook her head.

I wondered what Camilla Watson's ideal world would look like.

"I was a dreamy girl like you, once upon a time."

Her words stiffened the hairs on my arm. "Mrs. Watson, I—"

"I know my husband can be . . . harsh," she whispered. "But he was—*is* a good man."

"I'm sure he is," I agreed weakly.

"It isn't his fault," she said, as if trying desperately to convince herself more than me. Then she clasped her hands together and sat up straight. "I know you don't particularly like him, dear."

"Not really my place to judge either of you," I said honestly.

"Believe me," she said firmly. "I used to think that things could be different . . ."

I was uncomfortable and fully lost for words.

"But the truth is, they all turn out the same. Between work, family, bloody *life* . . . everyone needs a vice these days." Her voice was no longer melancholy but bitter.

"What's your vice?" I asked quietly.

She stared again at the blank wall in front of us.

"We let soldiers stay here during the war, you know."

"I didn't realize that," I replied.

"Most of them were young men—around your age I guess."

A subtle sparkle returned to her eyes.

"There was an older soldier too," she continued. "Jim."

I couldn't help assuming that *Jim* was her vice.

"And what happened?" I asked gently.

A sudden creak above startled us both.

"You should probably go back to bed, dear. Sorry to keep you up."

Her cheerless voice echoed in my head as I stood up to take our tea mugs to the sink.

"Lia?" Her eyes looked distant, like she was reliving another memory.

"Yes?"

"I love my boys."

"I know you do, Mrs. Watson."

"Please . . . please don't tell anyone about our chat?"

I nodded slowly.

"Now go back upstairs and dream about something good." She smiled faintly.

I paused at the stairway, feeling sad. She seemed so lonely, so conflicted about where life had taken her. As I ascended the marble steps, I wondered if those were the thoughts that plagued Camilla Watson's mind at night.

As days passed, I thought less and less about my odd encounter with Mrs. Watson. My focus shifted to classes and the abundance of material assigned each day. I left the withdrawn student of my past behind, making an effort to take interest in the knowledge at my fingertips.

One morning, I shuffled into my economics course and took a seat in the second row. The room quickly filled up as my watch hit the ten o'clock mark. This wasn't my favorite topic, but I'd done all of the required reading and wanted to prove myself in class.

Toward the end of his lengthy lecture, Professor Charles began asking questions. I perked up and set down my knobby pencil.

"What does the law of diminishing returns indicate?"

I sat in silence for a moment before lifting my hand into the air. I knew the answer.

The professor looked at me hesitantly before his eyes darted in the opposite direction.

"Anyone?" he begged.

I strained my arm and raised my hand higher.

"Anyone at all?"

I looked around a sea of suits and blank faces. No one else was volunteering, so why wouldn't he call on me?

"Ahem." I cleared my throat in hopes that the professor would notice.

After two infuriating minutes of silence, the professor dismissed the class.

"I suggest that you *all* study before our next meeting," he said, his eyes blinking behind a pair of wiry spectacles.

Unsatisfied, I gathered my books and marched to the front of the room. After everyone had left, I confronted Professor Charles.

"I know the answer," I said.

He didn't even look up from his reading.

"Didn't you notice my hand?"

The professor slowly met my intense stare.

"Miss . . ."

"Cole," I clarified.

"Yes," he said sarcastically. "My class is for students of the university. *Proper* students."

Stunned, I searched for a decent response. "I'm here taking classes—"

"Look, Miss. I really don't have time for your questions right now."

"But I don't have any questions. I—I'm trying to tell you that I knew the answer."

He put up a pasty hand and waved me away distractedly, returning his focus to his reading. I walked away bemused, wondering why he had been so dismissive. As the classroom door shut behind me, I told myself it was because I was an American. It wasn't until later that I let myself realize that nationality had nothing to do with it. I had been ignored solely because I was a woman.

※

DESPITE my best efforts to ignore that incident, it remained at the forefront of my mind. A week passed as I moved through a monotonous cycle of classes, homework, and flyer-making. I resented the tedious work that was sending me into boredom once again, though Scarlett assured me that things would change after midterm exams ended.

"That's when we're presenting our case to the school board!" she told me excitedly over a late dinner one evening. "As long as they okay our preliminary proposal, we've got a shot."

We had taken to eating during odd hours so we could discuss our plans in peace. The west dining hall was always deserted late at night.

Now that I knew more about Oxford's history and previous policies, I felt comfortable speaking up. "Scarlett, I don't mean to sound cynical, but haven't several proposals already been submitted in the past?"

She pushed around her mushy green peas and soggy potatoes before looking up at me. She was just opening her mouth to answer when we were interrupted.

"*Well well well*, what have we here?"

A burly upperclassman—a rugby player—was making his way toward our tiny table with a friend.

"Looks like two pretty girls eating dinner where they don't belong," the other boy said.

The taunting tone of his voice sent shivers down my neck. Female students usually ate in the east dining hall. Suddenly they were sitting on either side of us. I shifted uncomfortably in my seat, trying to figure out what to say.

"What's your name, sweetheart?" asked the breathy voice next to me.

"Amelia," I answered quietly.

"A-me-lia." He winked as he imitated my accent. "I like American girls. Whaddaya say we take you both out for a drink?"

"We were just going," Scarlett said quickly. She reached for her brown book bag, and a stack of pink flyers fell out of the side pocket.

"Shit," she muttered under her breath before reaching to pick them up.

"Not so fast," the burly one commanded. He grabbed Scarlett's arm, which instantly made me ten times more uncomfortable.

I looked around for help, but there were no other bodies in sight.

"We've got ourselves a couple of bitch protesters, don't we, mate? The women's movement . . ." He read off the flyer before crunching it up in his meaty hand. "This is a load of rubbish."

"If you'll just let go of my arm, we'll be on our way," Scarlett said.

"I think we need to teach these two a lesson," his friend insisted. "Can't have any stupid girls running around our school, can we?" A toothless grin spread across his pudgy face.

As the rugby player yanked Scarlett's hair, something in me snapped. I realized that I had two choices: run or fight. I chose the latter. Before I knew it, I was hurling dishes, silverware, and heavy textbooks in their direction . . . anything to make them leave. Their expressions went from amused to scared in seconds.

"Mate, that one's crazy!" the fat one said. "Let's get the hell outta here!"

And then they were gone. I was laughing with relief as I turned toward Scarlett, but she stared down at her lap, long blonde locks covering her face.

"Scarlett?"

Her response was barely audible.

Without hesitation, I gently moved her hair so I could see her face. "Are you okay?"

"No," she whispered after a long pause. "No, I'm not."

"Did he hurt you?"

"That was nothing," she said under her breath. "But it took me back to a very dark place."

"Please tell me," I encouraged her.

The next five minutes changed my view of Scarlett Daniels forever. She told me something I never expected to hear.

"There was a girl I knew back home. Lucy." Scarlett's eyes smiled when she said her name. "The two of us were inseparable—we grew up together. And during our final year of boarding school . . ." She broke off, still staring into her lap.

"Yes?" I asked softly.

"It became something more."

It took a moment for me to understand what she saying, but eventually I did.

"It wasn't quite love, but I was very fond of her. When you've known someone your whole life . . ."

"I understand," I said, placing my hand on hers.

"We were walking through a park two years ago," she continued. "Lucy was about to leave for Paris. She'd always wanted to go . . ." Scarlett's eyes lit up once again. "Anyway, she gave me her bracelet and said to keep it safe until she got back."

I looked down and stared at the delicate sterling cuff on Scarlett's left wrist. It was inscribed with an L.

"A group of young soldiers were drinking in the park. They started saying things as we walked by. *Awful things.* I told Lucy to keep walking, but she was always so hardheaded." A half smile crept across her lips but faded quickly. "One of the men grabbed us. He got really physical. Lucy pushed him hard when he did and . . . his friend pulled out a knife."

Scarlett was in tears now. I didn't know what to say, so I held her hand tighter.

In between sobs, Scarlett spoke her final words. "He. Hurt. Lucy." The tears flooded her green eyes and rolled down her flushed cheeks.

"She's gone, Lia. My friend is go—"

My navy peacoat muffled her choked sobs as she cried into my shoulder.

And there it was: another contradiction. Just when Scarlett Daniels seemed like the strongest, luckiest person on earth, I met a completely different side of her.

Chapter 5

Weeks came and went like tourists taking a holiday. There were frequent meetings and more class assignments than I could sanely handle. I was waist-deep in study materials as exams approached.

I was tempted to withdraw from economics after the incident with Professor Charles, but forced myself to finish out the class. None of my other professors had been so obvious about my presence being unwanted. Maybe they just didn't care enough. I tried to pour all my energy into studying, hoping that it would help ease my frustration. The stuffy library became my home until the first round of dreaded midterms ended.

I walked home one Friday night after a late mathematics review. As I unlocked the front door, I wondered if anyone was still awake. All of the downstairs lights were off, so I crept into the kitchen and set down my book bag. I found a heaping plate of leftovers on the stove, labeled with my name in Mrs. Watson's unmistakably pristine handwriting.

I unwrapped the dish and smiled at her kindness. We hadn't really talked since that strange night in the reading nook. I hoped that she trusted me not to say anything; *of course* I wouldn't tell Mr. Watson. I still wasn't entirely sure what to make of our conversation, but a large part of me *did* feel bad for her.

I hadn't taken a second bite of pot roast before I heard a loud noise upstairs, followed by a frantic murmuring that was masked by the distance and the closed bedroom door.

"For fuck's sake, Camilla," Mr. Watson's voice boomed.

Then there was angrier talking and some shouting.

"Go get me another damn drink!"

Something glass shattered above me. I immediately stood up, filled with a sense of urgency.

"Please don't wake the boys," a timid voice begged.

I thought I heard a bang, but it was impossible to know for sure. And then there was silence.

NOVEMBER pumped new life into my schedule as vibrant colors crept onto the forest trees. I found myself outside more, taking morning walks and hiking with Scarlett and Will. The fresh air cleared my head and was a welcome change from the library.

Scarlett never mentioned the eventful evening we shared in the west dining hall; in fact, she seemed happier than usual, as if it had never happened. I alluded to her story on a few occasions, but she always brushed it off.

Late one night, Scarlett and I went to Wonderland to catch up and sip wine. Will was at a party and the place was empty, so I decided to broach the subject once again.

"Scarlett, I've been thinking more about your friend, Lucy . . ."

"I'd rather not talk about any of that," she was quick to respond.

"But—"

"Christ, Amelia. There's nothing to talk about." The color drained completely from her face.

"Does Will know?"

The room was silent until she finally spoke again.

"No. And there's no need for him to."

"Don't you think—"

"I said I don't want to talk about it!" she snapped. "Can't you respect that?"

"Fine." My tone was anything but apologetic.

Another painful silence surrounded us. All I could hear was the warm crackle of the fire in front of us.

"Look," she said, the sharpness gone. "I'm sorry. I get like that sometimes when I have my guard up. I'm angry, that's all."

"You have every right to be angry. But I'm just trying to be your friend here."

"I know you are. You're a good friend, Amelia. I need to be a better one."

"You and Will have been great to me," I disagreed.

"Ah, Will. The lady charmer." Scarlett chuckled under her breath.

"What do you mean by that?"

"Well, he's sweet and very easy on the eyes," she said with a wink.

"I like Will because he's kind. And good to you, Scarlett. Nothing more."

"God, Amelia. Don't worry. I'm not accusing you of flirting, if that's what you're getting at."

"I didn't . . . that's not what I—"

"He's unfaithful," she said flatly.

"What?"

"Doesn't sound like *dearest* Will, right? Oh yeah, believe it. Caught him twice last term and once over the summer."

"God, Scarlett. I'm so sorry."

"Don't worry. We have an arrangement."

"An *arrangement?*" I was under the impression that only troubled married couples could say that. But she changed the subject before I could ask more about it.

"So what about you? Is there a bloke back in America?"

"Kind of," I said as an image of Robbie danced through my head.

"Ooh la la! Do tell."

"His name is Robbie . . . I met him through my parents. We spent most of last fall walking through the orchards and—"

"Having all sorts of salacious encounters?"

"Scarlett!" My face must have turned beet red.

"Don't be such a prude." She laughed and adjusted the fur throw under her feet.

"I—I've never." Embarrassment flooded my body as I struggled to think of another conversation topic.

"You're lying!" Scarlett's emerald greens lit up as the fire crackled louder.

"Anyway . . ." I said loudly.

"Nice try! You're not getting off that easy."

"Scarlett, really . . ."

"You're telling me that Miss Amelia Cole is a bluenosed virgin?"

"You're just trying to embarrass me to death, aren't you?"

"Of course not! Lia, it's *me* you're talking to. We're practically best friends, for heaven's sake."

The genuineness in her voice relaxed me. Scarlett had so many friends, but it was comforting to know she felt the same way I did. She was the only person I wanted to spend time with those days. In a way, I thought of her as different than just a friend.

"Well, I don't know about you British women, but in America it's perfectly normal to save yourself until marriage."

I took a sip of my mulberry wine as Scarlett spit hers out.

"You honestly think that unmarried American women aren't having sex?" she cried. "That's outrageous!"

"No. What's *outrageous* is expecting everyone our age to have a long list of sexual encounters."

I sounded so much more defensive than I intended. Scarlett noticed this and eased up a little.

"Well, have you ever wanted to?" she prodded gently.

"No," I lied.

"Not with anyone? *Ever?*"

"No."

That was a bigger lie.

"Maybe we should get you to meet some blokes here, hmm?"

I shrugged.

"Let me think . . ." She tapped her shiny red nail against her bare lips. The glow of the fire only made her more beautiful. I sometimes caught myself staring at her for no particular reason.

"Got it! Marshall Riley, Will's mate. He's perfect!"

"Who?" I sounded almost as uninterested as I felt.

"Trust me, you'll like him. The four of us can go to the December Ball together! Like a double date."

"Scarlett"—I was ready to switch gears—"why haven't you been in literature class lately?"

"Oh, I forgot to tell you! Someone's asked me to be in the winter production! They're doing *Romeo and Juliet.*"

"You're kidding!" I didn't even know that Scarlett liked acting.

"I've been doing drama on the side since I've been here," she explained. "It's an incredible opportunity . . . you know, for acting and modeling in London."

"I can imagine you doing that someday if you really want to."

"Really?" she smiled. "Thanks, Lia. You're too sweet."

I blushed and told myself it was the wine.

"Well there aren't a lot of other options, are there?" she asked cynically. "I sure as hell don't want to leave Oxford just to become someone's housewife . . ."

"You *don't?*" I teased. "But that's the dream!"

We both giggled and sipped more wine. It was the reality, though. Most women would get married young, stay home, and raise a family.

Chapter 6

SCARLETT

She has this way of permeating my guard. Amelia just slithers through—bit by bit—without me realizing. By the time I do recognize what she's doing, I'm usually too late. My defenses are down and I'm forced to overreact. It's vexing, really.

The thing is, I don't even think she's doing it intentionally. She's naturally curious, but it's more than that. Amelia treats me differently than I'm used to. I've actually come to think of her as one of my best mates, a true confidant.

We see each other regularly, usually at hangouts initiated by yours truly. I don't mind it, really . . . *Lia*—she likes when I call her that—is just painfully shy compared to me. Then she invites me to *Wonderland* for *tea*, which has come to mean *wine*, and of course I agree to join her. We're drinking and talking and I'm getting a warm flush. Then she mentions Will and I almost reveal everything. I stop drinking before I'm burning with a blue flame. Tipsy Scarlett isn't great at keeping secrets.

Chapter 7

LIA

It was Thursday, a mere twenty-four hours before we were to present our proposal to Oxford University's board. Unexpected December sun shone on my face as I stared out the window. I took it as a sign of good luck. I was done with morning classes and manning our information table in the quad. We hoped to get last-minute supporters from the pool of students that frequented the area at lunchtime.

A sharply dressed professor approached our table. I recognized him from my Tuesday history seminars—he taught across the hall.

"Hello, Professor!" I said, attempting a friendly greeting.

But there was no response as he walked faster toward us.

"Hello, sir," I tried again.

Still nothing.

Before I could venture another try he was towering over me, glaring down through his thin-framed glasses.

"You ought to be ashamed," he snarled. "Women don't belong here, period. And here you are trying to bloody graduate!"

I was lost for words. It was the opposite reaction I would expect from a professor. Ignorant students, *maybe*. But esteemed faculty? *Definitely not.*

My eyes followed him as he walked away. He approached a group of male students clustered around the science building and as he spoke to them they kept glancing over, making me feel uneasy.

It wasn't long before several of them approached my tiny table. I sat up straighter, preparing to shoot back witty statements when they started egging me on. But to my surprise, they didn't say a single word. Instead, they spread out around the table with their backs to me. Soon they had formed a complete circle, blocking my view of the students walking by. I realized that their true intention was to prevent any students from seeing *me*.

A few of them glanced over their shoulders and sneered at me. Others made derogatory comments under their breath, just loud enough for me to hear. I was trapped, stuck in my trivial chair as these men towered over me. I felt my throat tighten as I tried to come up with a plan.

Then I saw movement in front of me, and suddenly Scarlett was there, shoving men out of the way and forging a path to the table. They looked stunned, as if they didn't expect a petite blonde to push back.

She took a seat next to me and gave my hand a quick squeeze.

"This is crazy . . . I think we should go," I whispered.

"What are you talking about?" She looked at me like I was insane.

"They obviously don't want us here, and there are a ton of them, Scarlett!" I hissed. My nerves were getting the absolute best of me.

"That's what this movement is about. You think we'd be doing all of this if they wanted us here?"

"I know, but we're supposed to see the board tomorrow and I want us to make it to the meeting in one piece." I was half-joking, half-serious.

"Amelia. You have to be brave." Scarlett looked me straight in the eyes.

"I don't understand the point of all this," I muttered under my breath. "It keeps getting us into trouble."

"The point? *You know the point.* We'll be able to graduate with those men someday," she said firmly. "We'll be their equals."

"You sound so sure."

"I am sure. So long as women keep believing in themselves."

That was one of the things I loved about Scarlett. Despite the crimson lipstick and traditional clothes, she was unlike any woman I knew.

THE dim evening light was just enough to illuminate the windy path in front of me. I had stayed late after mathematics class to ask a few questions, and was late to meet Scarlett. *Again.*

I thought about what we would do that night at Wonderland. *Practice our presentation, gossip, sip wine.* Those private meetings had become the most exciting part of my schedule.

I noticed a group of men as I made my way through the woods. They were huddled around a fire pit, joking around and talking indistinctly. A couple of them looked over when I tried to stray from the path.

"Hey," someone shouted as I picked up my pace.

"You there! Pretty girl!"

I put my hood on and stuck my hands in my pockets. I knew they would stop if I ignored them. The others murmured something, and then loud footsteps were trailing me.

"Stop!"

I didn't let myself turn around.

"I said stop, bitch!"

His voice was much more aggressive than before. My breath quickened as I stumbled over fallen branches.

"Where are you going?" he shouted as I broke into a full run.

Chills were running down my back now, and I wasn't sure if it was the cold air or the impending threat behind me. Two hundred yards out, I was gasping so loudly that I could barely hear his footsteps.

Finally, I stopped, sure that I'd lost him. I looked up at the sky and took a deep breath. The gentle gray of dusk had intensified to a smoky blue.

"There you are!" A forceful shove sent me to the ground, and my book bag slid off my shoulder.

Shaking, I rolled over and faced my attacker.

"Filthy American," he sneered. "Go home."

He had a squinty face with bitter blue eyes. As I registered his shirt and trousers, I realized that he was one of the protesters from that afternoon. I stood up and dusted off my palms.

Every fiber of my being told me to punch him, to hurt him—badly, if possible. But instead I hurried away as he shouted unthinkable things in my direction.

I never told Scarlett about what happened that night. Maybe I didn't want her to worry about me. Or maybe I just didn't want to acknowledge the fact that I fled when I should have fought.

FRIDAY morning finally came. The sun was hidden behind swollen gray clouds and I was a bundle of nerves as I got ready for our big meeting. I put on every smart piece of clothing Scarlett had picked out for me, stopping only to admire how businesslike I looked. But I still couldn't shake thoughts of what had happened the night before.

I met Scarlett, Ida, and Will outside of the administration building promptly at 7 a.m. We'd spent the previous night rehearsing everything backward and forward, taking turns pretending to be board members. Now, hoping desperately that it would pay off, we walked up the stone steps and through the daunting double doors. All I could do was take a deep breath, look straight ahead, and march into the university office like I knew what I was doing. Scarlett flashed a nervous smile and followed my lead.

TWO hours later and we were back on those stone steps. The entire meeting had been a blur. I wasn't sure if I had blacked out from excitement or sheer embarrassment. I looked around, hoping that my friends could fill in the blank spaces.

"You were brilliant, Lia!" Will wrapped me into a bear hug and kissed me on the cheek.

"Very impressive," Ida agreed dryly.

I waited for the only opinion I really cared about.

"That was . . . astounding," Scarlett finally added after a few moments.

I flushed red.

"Where did that come from?!" Will nearly shouted.

"I—I don't know . . ." I said honestly.

He grinned and shook his head. "So humble, Lia. So *bloody* humble."

But humility had nothing to do with it. I honestly had no idea what had just happened. Apparently, though, I'd done something good, even *brave*—according to my friends, anyway. As we all walked away in separate directions, I heard Will whisper to Scarlett, "Lia can be awfully quiet, but damn, she speaks up when it counts."

Later on they would tell grand stories about how I took charge during the meeting. That when the board initially rejected our proposal, I fired back with reasons why they should listen to what we had to say. Apparently I ran the discussion from there, but it just sounded so unlike me. I wondered if Will was right. Maybe I had developed a quiet strength that only came out when it really mattered.

The rest of my day passed easily as I rode out my presentation high. I walked back to the Watsons' after class, planning on an early night to catch up on sleep. My buzz was fading, and even the rosebush-lined sidewalk felt rough underneath my tired feet.

I looked up to see that the front door was ajar, and it stopped me in my tracks. It was getting late and the Watsons' car was still in their pebbly driveway instead of the garage. I hesitated for a moment before entering the mansion. I shut the door quietly behind me and tiptoed up to the staircase. There were only a few steps left when I heard Mr. Watson's angry voice booming from the master bedroom, "I bloody well know what it is, Camilla!"

Mrs. Watson's mild tone did little to appease him.

"Well, I don't want that filth in my house!"

Her voice grew louder but was still muffled from my position.

"Fucking women's movement. It's *garbage* is what it is," Mr. Watson growled.

I felt chills creep down the length of my spine as I inched closer to their door.

There was more inaudible talking, and then the door flew open and Mr. Watson was standing in front of me, hair disheveled, an empty glass in his hand, and a menacing look in his eyes. "Well, well," he muttered when he caught sight of me, and a toothy grin took hold of his face.

I stood frozen in place as Mrs. Watson peered over his shoulder. She flashed a horrified look in my direction before moving past him and placing herself in between us.

"Lia, dear," she said with a shaky voice.

"H-hi."

"Were you eavesdropping, girl?" Mr. Watson asked threateningly.

I shook my head and clutched my book bag even tighter.

"Maybe we should see if she knows anything about this nonsense," he said, glaring at Mrs. Watson.

"Bruce, she doesn't—"

"Shut it!" he barked.

Mr. Watson walked back into the bedroom, leaving Mrs. Watson and myself alone at the top of the stairs. She held her finger up to her lips and shook her head slowly. I wasn't sure what she meant.

"What is this?" he snarled as he reemerged from the room. "Is it *yours?*"

Mr. Watson held a crumply pink flyer in front of my face. His intense stare didn't leave my eyes until Mrs. Watson spoke.

"I told you, Bruce. A group of Oxford students dropped it by the house earlier today while you were at work."

I suddenly understood Mrs. Watson's gestures.

"It's bloody unacceptable!" he snapped as he turned back to face his wife.

"They were just canvassing the neighborhood," she said weakly.

"Listen, girl," he said, glaring at me again. "If this is yours, you better wise up. Because I don't tolerate this type of trash in my house."

I wondered if he could hear my heart pounding against my chest. Beads of sweat pricked the back of my neck, but I tried to appear calm. The moment reminded me of how I'd felt in the woods just weeks earlier.

"You don't know anything about this, do you dear?" Mrs. Watson prompted me.

Still frozen in fear, I wanted to tell them that I *did* know about the movement—that I was actually an integral part of it. But as I looked at Mr. Watson's face, I realized that everything would be wasted on him. His bigoted mindset was held up by years of experience and reinforcement. So I shook my head reluctantly and stared at the snowy white carpet beneath my feet.

Chapter 8

SCARLETT

That's the moment I realized it. *The presentation.* We're standing there with sweaty palms and red faces, awaiting the board's rejection, and then out of nowhere, Lia raises her voice. And she does it in the most fantastic way—not defensive, not offensive, just plain convincing. In that moment, she was confident as hell and impossible not to admire.

Of course Will loved it too, just for different reasons. He couldn't stop bloody praising her. I wonder if she remembers what I said that night at Wonderland. I wonder if I tainted her opinion of him. I told her that Will was unfaithful and who knows what else. Which is not a lie . . . not all of it, anyway. Technically, he *has* cheated on me. But with men.

I met Will at an underground club ages ago. We were young teenagers in London, drunk on secrets and fear. Then again, *secret* and *homosexual* go hand in hand. I just can't believe I almost told Lia everything. Will would kill me.

We have something special, he and I. It's not exactly romance, but it's a hell of a friendship. We take care of each other and maintain the necessary facade. As far as I'm concerned, Will and I *are* in a committed relationship.

That's why I've had such mixed feelings about Lia. Of course she's attractive, but it's risky for so many reasons. When I'm around her, I want to be dangerously honest. I want to tell Amelia Cole how often I think about her. I want to tell her that Will and I are nothing more than best friends. Most of all, I want to tell her that I've fallen in love with her.

Chapter 9

LIA

I never spoke another word to Bruce Watson. In fact, he left on a business trip two days after the incident and didn't return for the remainder of my stay. I'm still not sure what exactly happened between him and Camilla, but I didn't dare ask.

With the remainder of our team still on a high from the university presentation, we decided to call off meetings until the following term. Everyone agreed that it would be good to have a proper break and enjoy the holidays. The December Ball—a highly anticipated event that rendered most students giddy from pure excitement—was upon us. We planned to go as couples: Scarlett and Will, Ida and Ryan, Marshall and me. Although I was still uncomfortable going to a dance with a stranger, humoring Scarlett was too tempting to pass up.

I invited Scarlett over to get ready, capitalizing on Mr. Watson's absence and secretly hoping she would help me look half-decent. The night of the dance she arrived early, armed with a trunk full of British makeup and fluffy cosmetic brushes. She followed me upstairs, heels in hand and ball gown draped over her shoulder.

I shook my head and smiled, knowing that my ruddy complexion would give her a run for her money. But Scarlett was up to the challenge. A flurry of products transformed my skin, and I watched satisfaction creep onto her face as she worked. She lined my eyes with rich black kohl before dusting sparkly silver shadow onto my lids. When she was done I glanced into the mirror and gaped, wondering how my friend learned to apply makeup so flawlessly.

We both slipped into our dresses and giggled at the contrast. Scarlett's bright silver gown was every opposite of my black bodice.

"You look . . . stunning," she said, inhaling.

I smiled as she put on a pair of sapphire teardrop earrings. She held up a finger and fished through her evening clutch, then pulled out a diamond choker that made me gasp.

"For you," she said, grinning.

I walked toward her.

"Only for the night," she said with a wink. "It's my fanciest piece of jewelry."

I turned around and felt the weight of each stone as she fastened the band around my neck. We stood there for a moment, Scarlett inches behind me with her left hand resting on my shoulder. Once I got used to the feeling of her diamond necklace, all I felt was the weight of her slender fingers.

She played with the ends of my thick hair and murmured something about them looking tamer than usual. I not only heard but *felt* her laugh . . . a sensation of warm breath and ticklish vibrations. The strangeness of it all broke my captivation. I turned around and checked my wooden wall clock.

"Scarlett," I breathed. "It's time to meet up with the others."

We arrived as a large group then quickly split off into couples—after which Marshall, who was nice and quiet, immediately disappeared into a sea of tuxedos and ball gowns. I figured he was probably going to meet up with another girl and was surprised to find that I was relieved; my two left feet had been dreading a public display on the dance floor anyway.

The auditorium smelled of musky cologne and rum punch. Lively music played as drinks flowed freely. I looked around and quickly realized that my dark dress didn't fit in with the growing mass of vibrant chiffon evening gowns. Embarrassed, I said hello to a couple of classmates before stepping outside to inhale some crisp winter air.

As I walked toward the courtyard, I looked across the room and saw Scarlett. She was slow dancing with Will, head perched on his right shoulder. Her smoky eyes were cheerless, as if she was anywhere but in a room full of dancing college coeds. I smiled but she didn't see me. *Those sad eyes.* I stood there wondering why she looked so lost.

Eventually, I made my way into a rosebush-lined courtyard. I faced the frosty windows, staring at the enamored couples inside. Some were dancing, others laughing and talking. *How nice it must be*, I thought, *to feel that in love with someone.*

The corner of my eye caught a flash of Scarlett's silver dress.

"Hi you!" she said and hugged me quickly.

"Well, hello there," I said, attempting a fake British accent.

We both laughed as our collective breath turned to clouds in the shadowy air.

"Why are you all alone out here, Amelia?"

"Marshall left me for another woman," I joked.

"The bastard," she said, eyebrows quirking.

We both broke out into smiles.

"I don't really enjoy these things," I said. "To be honest, I always feel a bit out of place."

"So do I," she confessed. "I know it seems like I love these dances, but it's all a bit overwhelming . . ."

I looked up at her, surprised. Maybe there was still much more to Scarlett than I realized. We turned back to face the windows, staring silently into their glow for a while.

"The thing is Amelia, I only really want to dance with you."

Her unexpected words hung there patiently, waiting for a response.

When my stunned face didn't grant her one, she tried something else. Scarlett took my hand and led me beyond the ivy-clad brick buildings. Her silky palm wrapped around my hesitant fingers like a warm glove. Before long, I gave in to the tender sensation and gripped her hand like it was something I was afraid I would lose.

She pulled away once we reached a raised wooden gazebo. It was brilliantly decorated with twisted green vines. We walked up the stone steps until we were standing underneath it, lights flickering all around us.

As I admired the place we'd found ourselves in, Scarlett maintained a steady gaze on me. I pretended to be distracted, but she didn't let up until I looked back at her. My heart raced as I met her eyes.

"Amelia," she whispered and extended her arm. "Come here."

But I just stood there, frozen in place. "I—I can't," I finally managed to say.

She was all that I wanted in that moment. But I wouldn't let myself take one step closer to Scarlett.

"I know that I'm not the only one who feels this way," she said, moving slowly toward me.

"Please don't," I muttered inaudibly. The truth is, I didn't want her to hear me.

"You and me," she continued. "There's something here."

I turned away from Scarlett and stared into the darkness. Deep down, I knew that she was right. I'd denied my feelings from the day we met, hoping they would eventually fade. But they had only intensified, so I turned back to face her.

"Lia . . ." Her voice was a beautiful whisper.

"There *is* something more," I admitted.

"Does it scare you?" she asked hesitantly, moving even closer.

"Yes . . . very much."

We were face-to-face now, inches from each other.

"Does it scare *you*?"

"No." She smiled. "It excites me."

I took the final step, closing the space between us so that our bodies were just touching. All I could feel was the curve of her breasts, pressing gently into my chest. She leaned forward and planted a soft, sweet kiss on my flushed cheek. Her lips lingered there for a moment, and I inhaled her intoxicating scent. Then she moved back and looked patiently into my eyes. I smiled and leaned in, and her smooth mouth met my chapped lips—a heavenly contrast I wanted to bask in forever. Chills shot down my neck, and butterflies flooded my stomach.

"Was that okay?" she asked as we separated.

"Yes." I smiled. "*Yes.*"

All I could think about was how much I wanted to kiss her again.

She cast her gaze upward. "Look at the stars."

"They're brilliant," I whispered as I stared up into the twinkling sky. "I don't usually take the time to look at them."

"I can't *live* without a clear night sky," Scarlett whispered.

"What do you mean?" I asked.

"It's silly," she confessed. "But as long as I can see the stars, I know that everything will be okay. I just . . . believe in them."

"Like fate?"

She reached out and squeezed my hand tightly. "Exactly," she said. "Just like fate."

"Maybe it can be our thing," I proposed.

"Yes," she agreed. "You and me . . . we're like the stars."

That was the moment I realized I loved Scarlett Daniels. I would never again look at a night sky in the same way.

Our kiss lingered on my tingly lips for days. I felt like a frivolous schoolgirl whenever I thought of her. Admitting my feelings to Scarlett had also been admitting them to myself—and now I knew for sure that she felt the same way I did. That realization, and the concurrent excitement I felt, was enough to distract me from almost everything else.

Each night, I caught myself staring up at the stars. I snuck out onto the Watsons' balcony to look at the night sky and think about Scarlett. She had lengthy evening rehearsals, so we didn't see each other much the following week. But when we spoke in passing, she asked if I wanted to watch her act in the winter production. Of course I said yes.

Chapter 10

SCARLETT

"I love her."

"*Love?*"

Will looks at me through doubtful eyes. We're walking through a frozen off-campus park.

"Yes," I say—assertive, sure.

"Wow, Scar. That was quick."

"I know. But this is different. *She's* different . . ."

"I'll take your word for it," he says, winking.

"I'm serious, Will," I say, though I can't help but laugh.

"I believe you." He nods and squeezes my hand.

"I was thinking that maybe I should be honest with her."

I feel a tug as he stops walking.

"About what?"

"You know." I tilt my head.

"Scarlett. We have a deal."

"I know, but—"

"We keep this up until we graduate. *Your* terms, not mine."

I'm suddenly out of breath. "I have to go get ready. Rehearsal's at seven."

His stare burns through me until I turn away.

"Scarlett . . ."

"Yeah. I know."

He's still staring.

"I really should get to the theatre," I continue. "The play starts in a few hours."

"I'll be there," he says and gives me a quick peck on the cheek.

A group of students walks by, glances in our direction. Will sees them and instinctively pulls me in for a showy, lustless kiss.

Chapter 11

LIA

A set of red velvet curtains opened to reveal Verona, home of the Capulets and Montagues. Dialogue began and I was immediately immersed in Shakespeare's creative world. The costumes were as elaborate as the backdrops and stage props. A full house of theatre enthusiasts applauded each carefully-crafted scene and perfectly-cast actor.

Scarlett was breathtaking as she delivered her lines with unadulterated emotion. The audience felt her joy, lust, and eventual heartbreak as the last act ended. My eyes were glued to the stage until the final line.

For never was a story of more woe, than this of Juliet and her Romeo.

Everyone cheered wildly as the curtains closed and Scarlett disappeared behind a sea of red.

I *needed* to see her after that play. I left Scarlett a note backstage saying that I would stop by her room later that evening to celebrate, and practically ran back to the Watsons' to shower and fuss over my outfit for a while. After much deliberation, I settled on a lavender lace dress that flattered my slim frame.

I knocked twice before turning the brass knob. Scarlett often left her door unlocked.

"*Amelia*," she said with a shy smile. She was sitting in a large maroon armchair in the corner opposite the door.

"What's all this?" I smiled back. The room was aglow with vanilla candles and tiny red lanterns. Soft music hummed in the background. I glanced at Scarlett's shiny Victrola and grinned.

"I love decorating." She slipped off her rose-covered slippers and tucked her feet under her knees. "Like it?"

"It's wonderful," I said as I walked toward her.

I sat down beside her and hugged her tight. She smelled like cinnamon candy and her favorite floral perfume. "*You're* wonderful."

"So, did you like the play?" she asked nervously before pulling away.

"It was magical. You played Juliet to a T."

"Maybe we should call up the boys to bring over beer and help us celebrate . . ."

I gave her a pointed look.

"Or we could get some for ourselves," she sighed. "Most of the guys are cellar smellers anyway."

"But . . . I just want to be with you tonight."

"Well," she muttered. She stood up and walked across the room. "I don't know why."

"Yes, you do," I said.

"I just . . . I don't know how to talk to you anymore."

"Yes you do, Scarlett," I repeated. I walked toward her slowly and reached for her hand. She didn't pull away.

"It's just . . ." She wouldn't meet my eyes. "I liked being your friend."

"Aren't we still friends?"

She looked at me adoringly. "Yes," she said, and finally exhaled.

Scarlett was always the brave one between the two of us. But that night, I was much more forward than she had ever been. I *craved* her. I wanted to show her how much I loved her, every part of her. I held her face in my hands and looked into her green eyes. She was quiet for the first time since we'd met.

I paused for a moment, silently asking if what I was doing was okay. She smiled shyly back at me and ran her delicate hand across my cheek. Then I kissed her, hard and slow. It was a promise—a vow to her. In that moment, I knew two things. I knew that I loved her. But more importantly, I knew that I'd never love anyone else.

Tingles ran down my spine as she carefully unbuttoned my lavender dress. I slipped her silk camisole over her head and set it beside us. Pure, unadulterated intuition was my guide. I had no idea what I was doing, and I hoped that Scarlett wouldn't notice.

"Lia," she whispered. "I *love* you." She pulled me down gently and pressed her warm body against mine. I felt both of our heartbeats, rhythmically soothing me until I couldn't tell which was which. Her long blond locks cascaded over us as we kissed and touched and tasted one another. I was overwhelmed by her sweet, salty skin and that delicious cinnamon scent. We explored each other fearlessly in the candlelight, our bodies sticky and intertwined, spread across her four-poster bed as another pretty song filled the room.

※

WAKING up next to Scarlett Daniels was like having a dream that lasted far too long. I wondered how this had happened, how I could be so lucky. I watched her sleep for a while, visually tracing her silhouette, until her lids opened slowly, revealing those piercing green eyes that still made my heart skip a beat or two. Watching her expression was like replaying the night before. A huge smile spread across her face as she, too, realized that this moment was real.

"Let's stay here all day," she whispered coyly.

"Okay," I agreed. My gaze didn't leave hers for an hour.

"What are you doing for Christmas?" she asked, finally breaking the silence.

"Nothing," I said honestly.

My parents had written about a winter visit, but I told them that the long ocean voyage wasn't worth it—I'd spend future Christmases with them.

"Come to London with me," she said, smiling. "We'll have a little holiday of our own!"

"Sounds amazing," I said, grinning back.

How could I say no to her when she was the only person I wanted to be with?

Chapter 12

We caught an early-morning train on December 23. It was a quick ride, most of which we spent planning our secret little vacation. *Should we have dinner in the hotel, or try someplace downtown? Should we exchange gifts, or go shopping for them together? How long should we stay?*

The city was glitzy and glamorous, beyond anything I could have dreamed up myself. There were festive decorations on every main street, ladies walking around in shiny black heels, and shop windows aglow with holiday displays. Slender mannequins stood proudly in department stores and caramel aromas emanated from corner confectionaries. As Scarlett and I carried our trunks side by side, I decided I wanted to stay in London forever.

We checked into our hotel and changed into fancier outfits. Scarlett looked stunning in a sapphire gown with a jeweled bodice, while I went with a white silk shift dress and two strands of black pearls. Scarlett convinced me to get my hair cut at a ritzy salon nearby.

"Just a trim, though," I pleaded.

"Absolutely not," she teased. "We're in *London*. You have to take a chance!"

To my dismay, I couldn't come up with a decent reason to keep my waist-length hair. It was wild, unruly, and frequently neglected. *Why not try something new?* Chunks of wavy ends fell onto the floor as I watched Scarlett's face light up with satisfaction.

When she was done, the hairdresser spun my chair around slowly until I faced a large mirror. I gasped as I processed my new look. There I was with a chic new bob and makeup to match. My rouged lips and lined eyes made me look older . . . more sophisticated. I felt like a new person.

"You look . . . stunning," Scarlett said excitedly as we left the salon.

I couldn't wipe the confident expression off my face all night. After we went shopping for shoes neither of us could afford, we ate at a restaurant called Rules, where a pianist played elegant music as we enjoyed the most wonderful meal I'd ever experienced. Fresh rosemary saturated my taste buds as I ate roast chicken and creamy whipped potatoes. I could smell Scarlett's ginger pan-seared salmon from across the table, and I ogled it until she let me try some. She teased me for eating so much but staying rail thin. I didn't mind; anything to laugh with her.

"Can you believe that this place has been around since the seventeen-hundreds? It's hard to imagine," Scarlett mused. "Charles Dickens used to eat here!"

All I could do was smile as I took it all in. I was having an incredible dinner in a new city with someone I loved. I'd never been happier.

After dinner, we put on our winter coats and ventured

into the chilly London darkness. Tall lamps illuminated the streets as shop lights slowly turned off for the night. I looked up at the evening sky and stared at those stars we both loved.

"Do you think we could ever . . . you know . . ." Scarlett kept her eyes cast upward.

"Be together?" I finished her sentence.

"Yes," she said faintly.

"You don't seem to," I said, looking at her curiously.

"I'd like to believe," she said.

"I believe in love. And I believe in us," I whispered as I took her hand.

All I wanted to do was to hold her tight and kiss her. I had to stop myself from taking her into my arms right then and there.

"Lia," she breathed as she inched closer. I could smell her freshly washed hair and, as I turned toward her, I saw the outline of her face. My heart began to beat faster, and then I remembered where we were. I stepped back suddenly, before anyone noticed.

"It's dark," she reassured me. "No one can see us."

My head told me to take another step back. I knew that once she was close enough, nothing could stop me from kissing her—not fear, not judgment, not doubt. My head was right. *But my heart.* My heart made me stay.

And then we kissed. A kiss as raw and electrifying as our first encounter, the kind that leaves your head spinning and your heart hammering at the interior of your chest. I wouldn't pull away first. *She'll have to.* Otherwise, I was certain that we would live in that thrilling moment until the end of time itself.

Scarlett held my face in her hands until we finally split

apart. Although I saw nothing else, I did see her eyes. They were prickled with blissful tears and melted mascara.

"Now look at those stars and tell me that we're impossible, Scarlett. *I dare you.*"

"LIA?" she asked on our final evening as I was making a pot of tea. "What do you think of me?"

"What do you mean?" It was such an open-ended question.

"How would you describe me? To a stranger."

"I would say that you're the most interesting person I've ever met."

Scarlett's eyes lit up as she digested my answer. "That's sweet," she said. "But you really don't know me well enough if you find me that interesting."

"What do you mean?" I asked again, sitting down next to her.

"I'm actually quite boring." She took a long sip of her chamomile tea.

"Oh, c'mon," I challenged. "We've gotten to know each other pretty well, Scarlett."

She was silent for a moment, and then, staring into the porcelain cup between her palms, she said, "Tell me a secret."

I thought hard about what I could tell her. But I'd been so candid lately that I felt like she knew almost everything going through my head. Finally, I said, "Before I came here, I felt like I was pretending to be someone. Someone who lived for academics and would do almost anything to impress her parents . . . someone who wanted a husband and a big house . . ."

Scarlett put her hand on my shoulder. "When I first met you, I felt like you were maybe just trying to fit in. You know, blend into the crowd. But you're completely different now. You have strong opinions and spectacular things to say and . . . I'm proud of you."

"Your turn," I said, smiling.

"A secret?" she asked thoughtfully, tapping those pink lips with her pointer finger. "I don't think I could live without acting."

"Well, I could have guessed after watching your performance. You're so convincing!"

"I have to be."

"Of course, I mean the play would crumble if—"

"I'm serious, Lia."

"I know you are . . ." I didn't understand her sudden change of tone.

"I've been acting my entire life. Not in plays, but every single day."

"Every day?"

"I understood very early on how my family worked. We keep secrets from each other."

"What do you mean?"

"I mean that my aunt doesn't tell my uncle about the other man she sees every Tuesday night. And he doesn't tell her where he really goes on Saturdays. I lived with them you know, ever since I was a girl. I was well aware of what went on behind closed doors, so to speak. *Such provocative behavior for such a conservative couple.*" She said it in a mocking tone. "So I don't tell them that I like women, because it would ruin them. For once, they would have to confront the truth." There was so much anger in her voice.

"You're in a new place now," I said gently. "Surely you don't have to maintain that sort of front—"

"It's not just my family. It's *everyone*."

"Scarlett."

"The world feeds on secrets, Lia. People have these thoughts and desires, but they learn to suppress them and just . . . *exist*."

"We don't have to hide anything from each other," I said.

"It's hard to break a habit after you've been doing it for so many years. Why do you think I'm such a good actress?" She laughed and twisted her hands in her lap. "The fact is, Scarlett Marie Daniels is just a show."

"You have everyone fooled, Scarlett." I wasn't sure what else to say. She was hurting so much and all I could do was sit there, helpless, watching her suffer. "I think that you can do anything you want to," I said honestly. "You're beautiful and brilliant."

She looked at me and opened her mouth, as if to say something, but closed it again before the words could escape. Then she leaned into me and gave me a long and unexpected kiss. She stroked my back as I pressed my lips into her neck, and then she started to cry—soft tears that fell onto my cheek like raindrops. Despite everything she had just told me, I knew that this was real. *Our love, this moment, her sadness.* As Scarlett continued to cry, all I could do was try to kiss her tears away.

We lay side by side that night as I slowly drifted into a soundless sleep. Every time I woke up, I would visually trace her beautiful face. I'd start at her delicate forehead and move down to the slight curve of her nose, all the way to her narrow chin and slender neck. In the morning, I found her wrapped around me. I inhaled the sweet scent of her hair as thoughts from the night before floated through my head.

When she finally stirred, Scarlett looked at me with wide, unguarded eyes. I smiled at her until a knowing expression cloaked her face. Memories of our conversation put her back on the defensive, only evident in her changing eyes. It was a subtle shift, imperceptible to anyone but me.

※

OUR train ride back to Oxford was a quiet one. Scarlett and I made occasional eye contact, but she always looked away before either of us spoke. We'd shared so much over the past couple weeks, I didn't understand why we were suddenly acting like strangers.

The sudden sound of our train stopping was a relief. We barely exchanged two words as we descended to the platform, but before we parted to go unpack our trunks, Scarlett placed a gloved hand on my tense shoulder.

"I'm sorry, Lia."

"For what?"

"Last night. I don't know what came over me."

"You don't have to apologize. You were just sad."

"No. I ruined the trip," she said despondently.

"*Scarlett.* We got to spend Christmas in London. It was the best holiday I've ever had."

She just stared at the snowy ground beneath our feet.

"Because I was with you," I added quietly.

"You mean that?"

"Of course I do. What I said was true, you know."

Recognition flickered in her eyes. "Me too. I do adore you, Amelia."

Chapter 13

SCARLETT

London is magic on its own. The city's heartbeat simply cannot be matched. But being there with Lia, seeing it through her unmarked eyes, is entirely enchanting. I don't want to leave this place.

I find myself blissfully unaware around her. We walk the streets like girls in love, holding hands and kissing on dark corners. Of course I have my usual hesitations, but she pulls me out of the fortress I've built up. She breaks down my walls and reminds me to look up at the stars.

We're back in the hotel room on our last night and Lia's making tea. I ask her to tell me a secret, still working up courage of my own. *Scarlett Marie Daniels is just a show*, I say, trying to tell her the truth without really telling her. There's a wrenching in my gut and I'm dying to be honest about Will and me. But I can't betray him.

I like falling asleep with her arm around me. When we lie side by side, it's like getting to be together without the usual fear that accompanies daylight. I try to stay asleep for as long as possible, because waking up means that everything *before* Lia wasn't a dream. When I dream, she's my constant. Amelia Cole is my past, present, and future.

On that final morning, I feel the cruel morning sun creep onto my face. Lia is wide awake, watching me with innocent eyes. For a moment, I smile back, completely unguarded. But the moment is short-lived. Because I know when we return to Oxford, my walls will reconstruct themselves, and I'll find myself pretending once again.

Chapter 14

LIA

Robbie came to visit me two days later—a complete surprise, and one I didn't initially respond to well when I found him on the Watsons' doorstep.

"Aren't you happy to see me?" he asked when he saw the confusion on my face.

"Of course I am!" I cried, recovering from my shock and hugging him tightly.

He kissed me hesitantly, a skeptical look on his face.

"Let's get some tea," I said, threading my arm around his.

He nodded his assent, and I steered him toward a nearby café.

"How's your family?" I asked.

"They're fine," he said, forcing a smile.

I wondered if things were still as tense as they'd been when I left.

"Lia . . ." Robbie seemed to read my face easily. "It's okay to ask. We miss him every single day . . ."

"I'm so sorry about everything—*about Ben*," I said quietly. "I'm not sure if I ever told you that enough."

He reached across the table and set his hand on mine.

"Your parents are doing well," he said, changing the subject.

"Oh? That's good. I really don't write often enough . . ."

"Yeah, they're looking at new spaces to expand the restaurant to. I do think they'd like to hear from you though. The Watsons write every so often to update them."

"God. I can only imagine what kind of news Mrs. Watson gives my parents."

"Oh, Lia." Robbie laughed. "I'm sure the Watsons are nice."

"Mr. Watson is a real crumb . . ."

For a moment, I wondered if I should tell Robbie more about the real Bruce and Camilla Watson. *The people who seemed so perfect through the glass windows of their expensive home.* But I shook my head at the thought.

"But . . . they're fine," I shook my head.

"So tell me about Oxford," he encouraged with bright eyes.

We fell back into that easy conversation pattern we'd always had—one, I now realized, that I had very much missed since coming to England. I told him everything. About how I wanted to leave the second I arrived but forced myself to stay anyway. About the movement and my friends and our meetings. About speaking in front of the school board.

I told him about everything except Scarlett. I figured that lying to protect his feelings was worth it. We talked more about life back home, and I vowed to write more frequently. As the café emptied, Robbie moved his chair closer to mine. When we were the only two people left, he put his arm around me and leaned closer. I instantly felt something that I couldn't quite identify. I thought perhaps it was something left over from our transitory romance, but blocked by my overwhelming feelings for Scarlett.

As we sat there in conjoined silence, Robbie's comforting embrace sent me into a dreamlike haze, and memories of our time together flooded my head.

"I love this part," he whispers into my ear.

A black-and-white film flickers on the screen in front of us. It's late July, and we're the only ones in the cozy Brooklyn picture house.

"Me too," I whisper back.

He puts his arm around me and I feel the welcome warmth on my bare shoulder.

The main actor kisses his leading lady passionately onscreen. Instrumental music fills the theatre as they kiss again.

"You're the one," he tells her.

Robbie's hand tightens gently as I lean my head on his inviting shoulder. The screen fades to black and dim theatre lighting illuminates our row. We stay seated, relishing the romantic moment.

"Amelia Cole," he says.

I turn to look at him, our faces just inches apart.

"Robbie Wells," I say playfully.

His dark outline reminds me that my eyes haven't fully adjusted to the light.

"I love you," he whispers.

I turn back toward the wall, lost for words in every respect. A million things run through my head.

"You okay?" he asks.

I feel his expectant eyes burning into the side of my skull. I know I owe him some sort of response. But I can't say it back . . . I just can't. So I lean over the metal armrest between us and kiss his full lips.

The memory ended as I came back to the present. I turned

my head slightly and looked into Robbie's familiar eyes. Lucid and blue, they gazed back in a way that made me feel special. Maybe *this* was the right choice all along. We were easy and far less complicated than Scarlett and I would ever be.

But then he tried to kiss me, and I pulled away on impulse. Guilt overwhelmed my heart as I looked into his mystified eyes. I still cared about him so much, and in that moment, I knew that I needed to be completely honest. He deserved the truth.

So I forced myself to talk about Scarlett. I told him about falling for her and everything else. It was difficult to keep speaking as I watched his awareness register. I imagined how hard it would be to receive this news myself. He asked the occasional question, but mostly just listened intently.

After I finally got everything out, I took a deep breath. Robbie's eyes were inscrutable.

"Robbie?"

We both sat motionless in the silence.

"I came here to—"

"To what?" I asked.

"Never mind." He shook his head and stood up.

I watched him walk out of the café, leaving me behind as my feet tapped the crumb-covered floor. I felt like a real louse in that moment.

"Miss? We're closing now," the barista said.

I gathered up our cups and quickly returned them to the counter. Robbie faced away from me as I walked outside toward him.

"Hey," I took a deep breath and placed my hand gently on his shoulder.

He turned around, kinder eyes lighting up his face. Robbie stared at me for a while before cracking a slight smile.

"I can't say that I'm not disappointed," he said. "I guess I was . . . just off the boat."

"Robbie—"

"I'm proud of you, Lia. I just want you to be happy."

I felt a tug on my heart when he said that. Robbie's reaction gave me hope. Hope that other people might not judge us as harshly as Scarlett feared.

"What about your parents?"

"Haven't told them." I sighed. "They won't understand."

"You don't know that. It probably won't be duck soup, but they do love you."

"I'll tell them eventually," I said, not knowing if I ever would.

"And what about you and Scarlett? What are your plans?"

"I—I don't know. I can't imagine life without her. But I'm supposed to go back to New York after next term."

"But you love her," he said gently. "You have to fight for her."

"Do you really mean that?"

"Not yet." He smiled. "But I will."

My eyes met his, and I suddenly saw him in a new light.

"Robbie?"

"Yes?"

"I really hope we can stay friends."

He pulled me into another comforting bear hug. His crisp scent relaxed me, and I let myself collapse into his familiar embrace.

Chapter 15

SCARLETT

"How was London?"

I can't tell if he's genuinely interested or merely gauging my level of affection for Lia.

"Wonderful," I say as I pour us another cup of tea.

Will taps his fingers on my coffee table then leans back into the couch. He starts talking about this and that, but I'm not really listening.

I interrupt him midsentence. "I'm going to tell her."

He looks at me with an unreadable expression. "We've been over this." He sighs and rubs his temples.

"You're being selfish, Will. I won't tell her about *you*, if that's what you're worried about."

I know that it's illegal for men, and I would never ruin things for him.

"That's not the fucking point, Scar—"

"Well don't cast a kitten about it."

"It's not the bloody point!"

"Oh! Really? What is then?"

"You want to tell her about our fake relationship, and—"

"I just want to be with her!"

"You have no idea what could happen."

"*Christ*, I'm not going to tell anyone that you're homosexual. This is about me and Lia!"

"But what's the difference? It's not like you can tell the world that you're in love with a woman."

"And why not?"

"You'll get hurt, Scarlett."

I shake my head and look away. He's wrong.

"Don't you remember why we started doing this in the first place?"

I stare out the window as rain falls against smudged glass.

"We want to make a difference. You think people will listen to us after they find out? We've made so much progress with the university board!"

"Then I'll wait until they give us a decision."

"What about your career?"

"I can still act, Will."

"Who's going to hire you after this is public?"

I open my mouth, trying to form a response.

"And what about *Lia*?"

"I love her," I breathe.

"What about *her* life? *Her* dreams? If you really love Lia, you'll think about her too."

"I love her," I whisper again.

That's all I know for sure.

Chapter 16

LIA

Robbie's unexpected visit put me in a new state of ease. I begged him to stay longer—after all, he'd spent the past several days on a ship just to see me. But he said that he wanted to spend some time in London, the place where Ben died just a few years before. I almost felt guilty for not going with him.

After he left, I felt even more in love with Scarlett. With New Year's right around the corner, there was a sense of possibility in the air. But sneaking around was getting old quickly, and I felt uncomfortable whenever we were around Will. I realized that we needed to talk before we fell into a permanent pattern of secret visits and forced concealment.

"What are we going to do?" I asked softly one night, nuzzling Scarlett's neck.

"Mmm," she purred. "About what?"

"Us."

She was quiet for a while. "I mean, Lia . . . you know that this can't go any further . . ."

"What do you mean?" I pulled back from our lingering embrace.

"You know what I mean," she said gently. "We could never—"

"Never *what?*"

"No one can ever know about us."

"Is this because of Will? But he cheated on you!"

"This has *nothing* to do with Will," she hissed. "It's the world! Don't you understand?"

I told her about Robbie's understanding reaction, hoping it might put her at ease.

"Oh, *Lia.* He's just the rare exception to a universal rule," she said bitterly.

I inched closer as she moved back.

"I want to be with you," I said unapologetically. "I'm in *love* with you."

"And I'm in love with you," she cried.

"Then what's stopping you?"

"I—I can't," she finally whispered.

I felt unexpected tears welling in my eyes as her words sank in.

"Scarlett," I said, my voice strained. "Please."

For a moment I thought I saw a flicker of something pass through her eyes. But they quickly returned to their indecipherable state.

"I don't know what you want me to say," she responded sadly. "We simply can't be."

I thought about our recent night in London. She was turning back into that scared, cynical person who didn't want to risk telling the truth. I needed to change her mind.

"I'm trying to fight for you, Scarlett. Don't you see that I've transformed since being here? Since meeting you?"

"I do." She smiled through her tears. "You've really come into your own."

She was right. I was miles from the flimsy girl I had arrived as. I had chopped off my hair into a flapper bob, gained a sense of style, and learned how to apply makeup properly. But more importantly, I was stronger, bolder, and more confident. I'd found purpose as an activist, fighting for women's rights and equality. All while falling in love with the woman sitting next to me. The total realization conjured up more tears.

"Please, Scarlett," I begged. "I don't know what I'll do without you."

"You will always be the most important thing that ever happened to me," she said.

"If our love is so important to you then why aren't you fighting for it?" Salty tears flooded my eyes as she averted her gaze. "And everything we've worked for! Was it all for nothing?"

"You know it's important to me. You've become my life, Amelia."

"Then neither of us can be happy unless we're together," I choked out.

"That kind of thinking will only make you miserable," she said quietly.

She took me into her arms. "The world just isn't ready for us, my love."

"But what about the stars, Scarlett?"

Her only response was a slow, heartrending kiss. She didn't

need to explain; I knew exactly what she meant. The heaviness of it—the fact that it was bigger than both of us—somehow calmed me. We lay there in silence for a while, filled with a tacit understanding that we would have to endure, together or separately.

Still, I tried to figure out how things could work, how *we* could work. The moment was pure and bittersweet: holding the girl I loved and trying to reassure her that everything would be all right, but crying with her because we both realized that it wouldn't.

Chapter 17

SCARLETT

It's December 31, and the only thing keeping me sane is this party. Music blares as intoxicated college students laugh and dance between sips of cheap liquor and coffin varnish. It's too loud to hear my own thoughts, but I prefer it that way.

"Ten, nine, eight!"

They're shouting for the countdown.

"Seven, six, five!"

I set my cocktail down on a wooden side table and glance around.

"Four, three, two . . ."

My head turns dizzy as the countdown continues.

"One!"

And then it's the New Year. Will grabs my shoulders and kisses me swiftly. We look like any other couple in love, though my lips are lifeless to his touch. After Will's mandatory show of affection, he moves on.

That's when I see her across the room, holding two flutes of pink champagne and staring at me sadly. I walk toward her, struggling to swim though a drunken sea of warm bodies. Everything is blurred, a combination of cigarette smoke and my own wine-induced haze. When I finally reach the end of the room, it's too late. She's gone.

Chapter 18

LIA

My decision to leave Oxford early was not an easy one. In fact, it was the hardest choice I'd ever made. At the time though, it wasn't really a decision at all. I couldn't even fathom the idea of being in the same place as Scarlett for another day, much less another term.

As I stepped onto the slippery train platform, part of my heart begged me to turn around. The part that belonged, and would always belong, to Scarlett Daniels. But the piece that I kept for myself remained determined to leave. Our last encounter had irreversibly shattered my spirit, but I'd managed to salvage a tiny sliver from the wreckage. The rest was damaged, misplaced, and irrevocably in love.

Chapter 19

Wonderland, January 1920

SCARLETT

It's a dark, starless night in the woods, and part of me wants to turn around. There's so much energy inside my head—transitory thoughts and heavy regrets. The ache worsens as I make my way through the towering redwoods. I want to take it all back, the words and their cruel repercussions. But I can't . . . and I can't turn back now.

I strike the match before tossing it far in front of me, a split second of doubt and nothing more. With the simple flick of my wrist, one tiny golden spark transforms before my eyes. Beautifully ominous flames abound in seconds. Even if I did want to take this back, it would be far too late. The grounds are already brilliantly ablaze with inferno and chaos.

I walk quickly as my paranoia proliferates into a beast of its own. I'm jogging now, treading on the shrubbery I've passed a thousand times or more. It's so dark that I can't see my own fingertips, much less what's in front of me. But it doesn't matter. I know every fraction of this forest—every branch of every tree.

I'm far away from the fire now, but its blaring roar convinces me otherwise. I stop running and feel the sharp air mount in my chest, a piercing pain exacerbated by the cold. The sting makes my eyes water as I attempt to catch my breath. Moments later, I turn around to face the amber glow.

I feel numb as I stare into the flames ahead. *She's gone. Because of me.* Bittersweet memories of our time together flood my mind until the fire has wholly consumed the building. *We ended because of me.*

And just like that, Wonderland is no more.

Chapter 20

New York, September 1922

LIA

It was my final year at New York University. I never expected to finish college, much less in a city so close to home. But I was proud of myself for going back to school despite my mother's concerns. Mom was worried that I'd be wasting money and "getting into trouble" in New York. It's strange and a bit funny to think about what actually happened . . .

After leaving Oxford, I worked in my parents' restaurant for a few months. The benefits were twofold: I made some extra cash while being distracted from Scarlett and my Oxford heartbreak. My mother encouraged me to stay in Brooklyn indefinitely and find a nice man to marry. She didn't understand why I wouldn't want to settle down and have children; didn't I want someone to take care of me for the rest of my life?

My dear mother's plan was flawed for a couple of reasons. First, I'd actually have to find someone looking for that kind of commitment. Second, and more important, I had no intention of ever settling down. That didn't sit well with her, of course, and became the inevitable base of our never-ending argument.

In the middle of a particularly slow closing shift at Selena's, I overheard two students chatting about class. I couldn't help but listen to their conversation, and it reminded me what I was missing out on. That was the night I decided to go back to college.

※

So there I was, a university student earning good marks in almost every class. I was staying in a spare room in Robbie's city apartment, located in the heart of artsy Greenwich Village. Despite his generous original offer—a free stay, no strings attached—I paid Robbie regular rent with the money I'd saved from working at my parents' restaurant.

Our neighborhood was eclectic and unlike anything I'd ever experienced. Dynamic poets performed on street corners and local painters created vibrant street murals. I loved walking through the village and watching different artists work. I had always been more analytical than artistic, and it was freeing to see that there was another way to be.

Once the fall term began, I started hanging around at a local coffee shop called Sally's. It was quiet and homey, a good place to read and study. I'd lay my books out across the table and scribble notes on scraps of paper. It was usually empty, and nobody seemed to mind.

There were a few regular customers that started to recognize me, though. An older man sat in the back booth and chuckled every time I walked in with my crowded book bag, shaking his head as I sat down. It didn't bother me because I assumed he was as lonely as I was. I'd smile at him and give a little wave. The difference between us was that I had books to keep me company.

Usually I'd just order coffee so they wouldn't kick me out. Money was scarce, but the hot liquid and free refills warmed me up. I didn't dare ask my parents for help; I knew their finances were just as strained as mine.

I had the same waitress almost every time I was there, a young woman named Rebecca. She wore a blue collared dress with a frilly white apron and black Mary Janes, and had a nice smile and dark eyes.

"Coffee with cream?" she asked me one day with a wink.

I looked up from my notes and smiled. "Yes, please."

She came back moments later and set a porcelain mug in front of me. "What are you working on?"

I was surprised. Rebecca hadn't said more than a few words to me over the past month.

"It's a project for my political studies class. I go to college at NYU."

"That's neat," she mused. "A *university* girl."

"Something like that." I smiled.

Half an hour later, Rebecca came back with a fresh pot and asked, "What do you do for fun then?"

"Sorry?"

"I mean, how do you clear your head after all that studying?"

"Um." I laughed. "I guess I just go back to my apartment and sleep."

"That sounds . . ."

"Boring?" I finished her sentence.

She nodded and we stared at each other for a moment. Rebecca tucked a stray strand of hair behind her ear and smiled. Her wavy red mane was pulled back into a messy braid that reminded me of my own. I grew out my chic London bob right after leaving Scarlett—the hairstyle reminded me of her and our time together.

"More joe!" called the older man in the back booth.

"One sec, Morris," she called back, and returned her gaze to me. "You should come out with me tonight."

"Come out with you?"

"We can go to this nightclub on Fifty-Seventh. You'll like it there, trust me."

"I'm not really that sort of girl," I said honestly.

"C'mon," she urged. "Tell you what. If you really hate it that much, your coffee is on me next week."

I couldn't help but crack another smile. "Okay, Rebecca. I'll go out with you tonight."

"Call me Beck." She grinned before leaving to pour Morris another cup.

I spent that evening frantically searching through the mediocre rack of clothes in my tiny closet. Robbie came in mid-breakdown and failed to stifle a laugh. I shot him a particularly angry look, which just made him laugh harder.

"What on earth are you doing?"

"Nothing that concerns you," I snapped.

"It actually *does* concern me. I mean, look at you." He chuckled.

I glanced in the bedroom mirror and saw myself sitting miserably in a heap of unfashionable outfits.

"Also," he added, "you're raiding my apartment."

"*Our* apartment," I corrected him.

"Our apartment." He grinned.

Just then, an ugly yellow scarf fell from the top shelf onto my head, sending us both into a laughing fit.

"You're too funny, you know that?" Robbie laughed.

After our heart-to-heart at Oxford, Robbie and I managed to salvage a pretty decent friendship. We didn't talk for several months, but reconnected after I moved into the city. He showed me around and even offered up a place to stay, which I didn't accept until my landlord abruptly ended my lease in the middle of my first academic year at NYU.

Robbie and I still got along well and liked a lot of the same things. He loved exploring New York and seeing shows on the weekends. We never really talked about our previous relationship, or Scarlett, for that matter. Us living together was strictly platonic, and he knew that.

"What are you doing anyway?" he asked.

"It's this girl I'm meeting tonight, Beck."

A knowing expression took over his face.

"Not like that, Robbie. We just met!"

He raised a thick eyebrow.

"Look, we're going to a speakeasy. I need something to wear but all I have are old dresses and frumpy sweaters."

"Hmm." He looked around the room. "There's got to be something in this pile of—"

"Garbage?"

We both laughed again.

I met Beck at the diner several hours later. She wore the same uniform; her long red braid trailed the majority of her spine. The café was empty aside from a few lonely customers, as usual. She looked up from the register and waved when she saw me, her amber eyes twinkling in the low light.

She poured her last cup of coffee and punched out, then grabbed a purple purse and hurried outside to meet me.

"Sorry to keep you waiting!"

She gave me a quick hug, and I smelled fresh coffee on her skin.

"Not at all." I smiled.

"You look nice," she said.

I'd decided on a maroon dress I'd found at the bottom of my closet.

"Thanks," I said, hoping I was dressed appropriately. I still didn't know exactly where we were going.

We walked down the street as dusk gave way to darkness. Twenty blocks later, Beck pointed to a rundown building across the way. "That's it!" she squealed.

"That's where we're going?"

"It is!"

I looked back to see Beck taking off her uniform in the middle of the street. I was opening my mouth in objection, and then I saw the strappy silver dress she was wearing underneath. I cracked a smile as she untied her braid and shook out her mane of waist-length auburn hair.

She leaned down to grab a pair of black heels out of her bag.

"Clever," I thought out loud.

She stuffed the uniform into her bag and smiled. "How else?"

We opened a large door and walked into an empty lobby of sorts. It was dim and musty, with no more than an old flickering overhead light.

"Don't worry," Beck said, seeing my confused expression. "There's the elevator."

We descended two stories before arriving at our destination with a jolt. The cage doors opened to reveal a smoky room filled with golden lighting and loud blues music. It made my heart beat faster as I stepped out of the elevator and followed Beck's lead. Something bright caught my eye—a large crimson sign. *Mae's Underground*, it said. As we walked farther into the room, a group of scarcely dressed dancers came into focus. Their bodies moved to the music as a few lights flashed overhead.

"This is it," Beck whispered.

She nudged me toward a small stage occupied by a blond singer wearing tight pin curls and a red dress. The petite woman belted tunes twice her size as the band behind her struggled to keep up. I looked at the sweaty drummer and wondered where he worked during the day.

The singer winked at Beck before she steered me away and over to a shiny countertop.

"What'll you have?" she asked over the music.

"What?" I shouted.

"Never mind," she said, laughing.

I turned back to face the dance floor. It was filled with women and men, singles and couples. I couldn't tell how old everyone was under the dim lighting. I guessed about my age or slightly older.

"Here you go," Beck said as she placed a beer in my hand.

I stared at the cold bottle until its condensation made my palms wet. We were in the middle of prohibition, and I'd never been to a speakeasy before. The experience was equally strange and exciting.

I thanked her and took my first swig. The bitter liquid ran down my throat as I listened to the end of the song. It reminded me of the parties at Oxford and drinking too much with Scarlett.

"Thanks ya'll," the petite blonde projected loudly. Her distinct southern accent surprised me. "The band and I are thrilled to be here. We're yours for the rest of the night!"

Cheers and drunken applause filled the foggy room, and it wasn't long before another song took over. This one was slower, with a smoother rhythm.

"Dance with me." Beck reached for my hand smoothly.

I set my empty beer on the counter, and without hesitation let her lead me into the center of the mass of sweaty bodies on the dance floor. But I couldn't keep the anxiety off my face.

"Just be free," she said, smiling at my apprehension.

I watched her glide around gracefully, like a beautifully wild ballerina. She hummed as she danced. Surprised and a bit embarrassed, I glanced around at the other couples—no one was dancing like Beck, but no one was watching her either.

I finally gave in and started moving the way she did. Her almond eyes and chiseled face were mesmerizing as we danced to the next song. When it slowed down, she reached for my hand again.

"Beck," I said in a warning tone as she put her hands around my waist, and I looked nervously around the room once again—only to realize that nobody cared. Everyone was solely focused on the person or people they were with. It was like we were invisible, in the best way possible. Before long, we were swaying to the singer's addictive, velvety voice.

"Isn't this wonderful?" Beck asked when we finally stepped off the dance floor.

"Yes," I said, trying to catch my breath.

She took my hand and led me past the shiny bar, behind the club's stage. Suddenly we were in a hidden pocket devoid of smoke and sound—a disorienting change of atmosphere.

"What are you thinking?" she asked, looking into my eyes.

I wasn't sure what to make of Mae's Underground. It reminded me of somewhere I'd been before, only a happier, flashier, and more intense version.

"It's like a secret," I said.

Beck smiled slightly and reached into a hidden pocket in the wall behind the stage. She pulled out a skinny cigarette and a single, unused match. I watched as the orange flame illuminated her warm eyes and lit her cigarette.

"Do you like secrets?" She puckered her cherry lips and blew out the flame.

"I'm not sure," I said honestly. The silence continued to shock my ears.

"You're different," she said. "Different than most people."

I locked hazy eyes with her and shrugged my shoulders. We both knew what she meant.

"Yes," I finally answered. "Are you?"

Beck took a long drag of her thin cigarette. I watched patiently as she blew clouds of smoke into the dark underground air.

"Of course, Lia," she said playfully. "Why else do you think I asked you out tonight?"

She offered me the cigarette, but I shook my head. We stood in silence as she finished smoking.

"That's not all I do, you know," she said.

I looked at her expectantly.

"I mean I do more than just working at that diner."

"Yes?" I smiled.

"I write," she said quietly. "Poetry."

She reminded me of someone I'd met before . . . only happier, freer, and less complicated.

Chapter 21

New York, May 1923

After Mae's Underground, Beck and I went to several other private dancehalls and secret clubs. It was one thrilling experience after another with her. Unlike Scarlett, she was wild and fierce in her openness. Between the two of us, *I* was the nervous one. Her boldness and confidence were striking.

Beck was twenty-five, two years my senior. She had grown up on a farm in Wisconsin and moved to New York the day she turned eighteen. She never really spoke about her family; the most she would tell me was that she didn't want to rehash the past.

Between my strained relationship with my mother and Beck's estrangement from her family, we didn't see many relatives. My mom disapproved of almost every decision I made. Our never-ending fights took a toll on me after Scarlett, and I simply didn't have the energy or motivation to argue anymore. Our relationship deteriorated into a tacit understanding—an agreement that we wouldn't talk to each other beyond quick exchanges in public. These fake pleasantries allowed my mother to *save face* in front of diners and houseguests.

I actually still got along quite well with my dad, but it didn't matter. In fact, I barely went home after moving to the city. The only people Beck and I spent much time with were Robbie and his girlfriend, Vanessa. In a way, those three became my family during my time in New York.

Ness was nice but not saccharine-sweet. She was good for Robbie, especially when he started talking about enlisting in the military. He told us that he wanted to honor Ben's death in some way. He wouldn't listen to what Beck or I had to say, but he sure listened to Ness. She urged him to reconsider and transfer banks instead. He moved into management and quickly forgot about the military.

When things got serious between Robbie and Ness, she moved into our Greenwich Village apartment. The arrangement was fine for a while, but the three of us were cramped, to say the least. I vacated the apartment during my last semester and went to live with Beck.

Still, our foursome tried to maintain regular get-togethers. We went on a lot of double dates and even took weekend trips together. Student life gave me the flexibility to work odd hours at the campus library and go on impromptu adventures with Beck.

⁂

ROBBIE and Ness were vacationing in Connecticut for the weekend, so we rented a beach cottage. Although we lived together, Beck and I had never really been *alone*. Her roommate Laura was always home, aside from the one time she left us by ourselves for the night. But on that potential-filled evening, we ended up getting drunk on cheap wine and falling asleep early.

Although our closest friends were more than accepting of us, we knew the rest of the city wouldn't exactly understand our relationship, so we mostly just told people that we were best friends living together until we each got married. Even Beck's poet buddies didn't all know the truth.

The beach weekend would be our first real chance to be ourselves, away from the chaos of New York City. We stepped off the empty train car and walked to the cottage we'd rented. It was right on the border between street and sand. We unpacked our bags and spent the entire day strolling along the ocean.

As nightfall obscured the salty waves, I took Beck's hand and led her back to the cottage. We kissed fervently for what felt like hours before falling into bed. Tangled in sheets and damp clothes, we fumbled around before finding our way.

Beck was gentler than I'd imagined, somehow softer and more sensual. Still nervous as ever, I tried to relish the fact that I wasn't a virgin this time around. I ran my fingers through her long mermaid hair as she kissed every salty inch of my pale skin. That night, for the first time, I slept soundly next to the woman I'd come to love.

⁂

AS graduation neared, I struggled to formulate a post-college plan. I'd taken all of the necessary classes and excelled in most of them. But there I was, unsure of what I actually wanted to do for a living. Women had few options for actual careers besides staying home and raising children. Unless you were a performer like Scarlett, the job choices were usually teacher, secretary, or nurse. We won the right to vote in 1920, and that came with a lot more professional possibility—I hoped that even more careers would open up for women in the coming years.

Beck still worked at the diner, but she actively pursued poetry during her time off. I went to almost all of her readings, at little cafés near our apartment and studios across the city. Her enthusiasm for the craft inspired me. Sometimes her spirit reminded me of Scarlett's, but I immediately tried to shrug off the thought each time it occurred to me. Since starting my job at the campus library, I'd become very interested in reading and writing. But I was convinced that most writing positions were reserved for men during that time.

Now that I was about to graduate, I wondered what would come next for Beck and me. Daydreaming had gotten me into trouble once before, but I couldn't help it. Beck was my confidant, my lover, and my reason for staying in the city. I couldn't really imagine life without her by my side.

※

"AMELIA Cole," called the announcer behind the podium.

I stumbled awkwardly across the stage. I looked out into the crowd and saw hundreds of faces, some smiling and others indifferent. Beck, Robbie, and Ness waved from a few rows back, which made me beam as I shook the dean's hand. I glanced back into the audience and saw another set of waving hands. To my shock and disappointment, they belonged to my parents.

The reception following our ceremony was filled with proud spouses and supportive families. I moved through the crowd to find Beck, but ran into Robbie along the way.

"Did you know my parents were coming?" I asked him quickly.

"Course not," he said, hugging me. "But congrats, Lia! Can you believe it?"

I didn't have time to answer before Ness surprised me with a tight hug. "We're so, so proud of you."

They stood side by side, looking like the perfect American couple. I wondered when they would finally get married and start a family. I could see that future written on their faces.

"Lia, honey!" called my mom's unmistakable voice.

I flashed a look at Robbie and whirled around.

"Mom, hi." I forced a smile.

My father trailed behind her, sweating in the New York heat.

I hugged them both before offering a pathetic explanation for why I hadn't invited them to the ceremony personally.

"We had to call the department ourselves, Amelia!" my mom complained. I guess our little standoff didn't leave room for missed graduation ceremonies. I'd forgotten that my parents even had a telephone—Beck and I still hadn't purchased one for our apartment.

I opened my mouth to respond as Beck emerged from the crowd. She flounced toward us, wavy red locks falling around her waist.

Conflicting thoughts raced through my head as we embraced, and I pulled away quickly, worried about what my parents would think.

"Mom, Dad. This is . . . my *friend*, Rebecca Hart."

"Pleasure to meet you," they said simultaneously, and each shook her hand.

As I looked at Beck's disappointed face, the moment turned into one giant flashback. I'd complained for months about Scarlett keeping us a secret, and now I was doing the exact same thing to Beck. I couldn't even tell my own parents the truth. Beck had every right to be upset. I was the Scarlett to her Lia.

Unfortunately, the remainder of our day was tainted by that critical moment. My parents took us all out for an early dinner, which mainly consisted of them encouraging me to move back home. I sweated bullets the whole time, wondering if Beck was going to blow my cover. She didn't, of course. But as my parents left, she was cold to me in a subtle way unnoticeable to anyone but me. We slept on separate sides of our shared bed that night, each wondering what the other was thinking.

LATER that week, Robbie called me out on my behavior at the ceremony.

"I think you really hurt Beck's feelings," he told me over coffee.

"What was I supposed to do? I had no idea they were coming!"

"She's your *girlfriend*, Lia."

"Exactly," I said. "They would disown me."

"You should be proud of your relationship . . . or at least be honest about it."

"Easy for you to say," I countered. "You and Ness are perfect for each other."

"I can't wait to marry her," he said smiling.

Relieved that I'd distracted him from the topic at hand, I opened my mouth to ask when he was finally going to propose. But he got right back on course before I could ask.

"She's good for you, Lia. I haven't seen you this happy since—"

"Oxford?"

He nodded slightly.

"That was different," I said quickly.

"Was it?"

His question hung in the air.

"Of course," I finally responded.

We sipped coffee in silence until Robbie spoke again.

"Do you think she's *the one?*"

I stared at him, wondering whether or not it was a loaded question.

"I'm not sure if I believe in that anymore," I said quietly.

"I do," he said. "And I think you do too."

I thought about our conversation the entire way home. Robbie was right. I still did believe in soul mates. If I could talk Beck into forgiving me, maybe we would have a shot at something more—a real future together. *Something little girls dream about at night.*

Chapter 22

Connecticut, June 1927

The pianist's elegant fingers moved swiftly over a set of polished black and white keys. A wonderful array of musical notes came together seamlessly as wedding music poured out of the instrument in front of us. Beck whispered something into my left ear, but I couldn't hear her over the distracting melody.

"Get ready to walk," she whispers again. "We can't screw this thing up."

"We won't." I smiled at my girlfriend in her rich emerald dress. Beck's fiery hair contrasted the gown's color perfectly. She was a stunning bridesmaid, to say the least.

"Places everyone," called a shrill voice behind us. It was Ness's over-particular cousin, Amanda. She had planned most of the wedding, including the orchestra and a decadent cream layer cake. "Oh come here, Ness! Stop fussing with your veil."

I shot a sympathetic glance at Ness, who was much too polite to tell her annoying cousin to fuck off. Instead, she walked quickly towards the corner where Beck and I were hiding.

"You look beautiful," I sighed.

"A flawless bride," Beck nodded in agreement.

"You two are liars," she laughed. "I can't believe we're actually getting married!"

"You're perfect for each other," I said and gave her hand a quick squeeze.

"No, *you two* are perfect for each other," she whispered.

I glanced nervously around to make sure no one else heard her comment. Ness winked at Beck and squeezed my hand back playfully. Her words carried more weight than she realized.

"We could, you know . . ." Beck said quietly as Ness walked away.

I couldn't even look at her. We'd had this conversation multiple times over the past year.

"Get married, I mean . . ."

I opened my mouth to reply as a cold hand shoved me forward.

"Walk!" Amanda commanded. "Follow her pace, Beck."

Wedding guests stared curiously in my direction as I fumbled down the aisle. I heard Beck's shiny heels trailing smoothly behind me and tried to correct my awkward steps. Red from embarrassment, I forced a smile as I approached the altar. And there he was—my best friend, standing proudly in a black tuxedo. He stifled a laugh as I nearly tripped, but flashed a reassuring smile at me before turning back to face the aisle. I finally stood still as Beck gracefully made her way over to me.

Ness's compliment replayed in my head as other bridesmaids lined up beside Beck and I. *You two are perfect for each other.* It was intended to make me happy, but it reminded me of a recurring argument between Beck and I. She had no doubts about our relationship and wanted to stay together until the end of time itself. While the sentiment was sweet, women couldn't live together as partners, much less get married.

Our situation was unique and only worked out because of our unwavering commitment to secrecy. I thought that Beck understood that, but our recent conversations had proven otherwise. My heart began to race as I thought about what might happen if she told anyone about us. I smelled the freesias in Beck's bouquet as I felt her frustration seeping through that emerald dress.

Every guest stood as Ness and her father emerged across the church. She was breathtaking in an ivory lace gown, straight brown hair flowing over her covered shoulders. I looked at Robbie and smiled at his reaction—he and Ness were blissfully content and irreversibly in love. It all seemed so simple for them, so easy to be together. Robbie took Ness's frilly veil in his hands and lifted it gently over her head.

Just then, I felt Beck's red waves skim my shoulder. I knew what she was thinking. She was wondering why that couldn't be us—why we couldn't have exactly *that* someday. My heart broke for her as Robbie and Ness exchanged their vows. I wanted to turn to her then and there, take her expectant face in my hands, and kiss her publicly.

"Robert Johnson Wells, do you take Vanessa Jane Quincy to be your lawfully wedded wife?"

"I do," he said.

"I do," Ness replied shortly after.

"I now pronounce you husband and wife. You may kiss your bride."

My best friends embraced as the audience swooned. In that moment, I wanted so badly to give Beck everything she desired. I wanted to, but I never could.

Chapter 23

New York City, February 1930

I closed the door to our roomy loft and hung up my peacoat. It was dark, with nothing more than moonlight to illuminate the apartment.

"Happy Valentine's Day," Beck said dryly.

Her voice startled me. She was sitting at the dining table with a dozen roses and an equally red glass of wine.

"Hi, darling." I smiled. "Didn't think you'd still be up."

I walked over to her, wondering why she was so dressed up . . . full makeup, with a sheer sapphire shawl draped elegantly over her shoulders.

"You look beautiful," I said.

"I got these for you," Beck said as she dodged my hug.

The red roses sat atop a handwritten card.

"What's wrong?"

Her heavily-lined amber eyes were cold and distant. "You know what's wrong, Lia," she said with a sigh. "It's been wrong for months."

I looked at Beck sadly, knowing full well what she was talking about.

"Your job is your true love," she said flatly.

"You don't mean that."

"I do," she shot back. "You've been avoiding me for months! Whenever we make plans for just the two of us, something always seems to come up."

"I'm sorry," I said, stalling. "But aren't you happy?"

"Are *you*?"

I was unhappy and I'm sure she realized it. We'd been together for almost eight years, most of them good ones. Through careers and hardships, we'd stayed as strong as we could. But loving someone doesn't necessarily mean you're meant for them.

"I love you, Lia," she whispered. "But it's obvious that you don't love me in the same way anymore." Tears pricked her striking eyes as the words set in.

"Beck," I pleaded. "I'm so sorry."

The gloomy look on her face only intensified. "It's awful," she choked out. "I thought we were meant to be."

I tried to hug her, but failed again.

"I know how this feels," I said. "I know how much it hurts."

"Then why would you do it to me?" she sobbed.

My heart broke for her as I tried to explain. "I didn't do this on purpose. It's just not that simple—"

She held up her hand to cut me off. "It's because of *her*, isn't it?"

I looked into her knowing eyes until she turned her head away.

"Beck . . ."

"Was anything actually ours?"

"What do you mean?"

She looked back at me and stepped forward so that our faces were inches apart. "Any of it. The things we did . . . the places we went . . . the way you kissed me?"

I opened my mouth and struggled for words.

"Your silence is enough of an answer."

"You and I—"

"Oh, Lia." Her voice softened. "You were half-loving me the whole time."

I looked out the window at the starless sky, wondering if she was right.

"You wanted me to fill some impossible void, when your heart wasn't even yours to give. It's always belonged to someone else."

"That's not true," I whispered. "And you're completely different than her."

"Exactly," Beck said with a sigh, and I realized that she was right.

I took her hand and paused for a moment. Her watery eyes reminded me of what I once lost. Beck started to say something, then shook her head and turned away. She picked up her glass and drank down all the wine in it before leaving the room.

I sat there for hours next to Beck's empty glass and the roses she'd bought for me. Regardless of what happened next, I could never unsee her moonlit tears.

⁂

BECK and I only exchanged a few words the following week. I felt guilty about breaking her heart after several years of what I had deemed a great relationship. But maybe she was right about us. Beck told me that my heart wasn't my own to give—something that I still didn't want to believe. Maybe I never should have told her about Scarlett and my time at Oxford. Maybe then, Beck would have been convinced that she was the only one for me. But wouldn't that have been a sordid thing to do? To convince her that Scarlett didn't exist—that my heart was untouched before I met her in that New York café?

Perhaps such a lie would have kept us together longer. Beck's insecurities would have lacked a base upon which to grow, to fester. What if she never even found out about Scarlett? She—*we* would have been happier. Life doesn't work that way, though. Love is permanent and enigmatic in its influence. Just as I would always love Scarlett, I knew that part of me would always love Beck.

I dwelled on that thought for several days before telling Robbie about us. He was shocked, but just as supportive as usual. Ness overheard our conversation and insisted that I come stay with them for a while. It was definitely a more tempting offer than the prospect of moving back home. But I felt a need to get out of the city—a place that reminded me so much of Beck.

At the end of that dismal month, my father drove over to pick me up. The entire situation felt like history repeating itself—a breakup causing me to move back home after I'd finally gained some autonomy. I stood by the window as my dad's car hovered on the busy street below. Beck was in the kitchen, busying herself and trying to avoid an inevitable farewell. I rolled my suitcase over to the entryway and picked up a pile of boxes that held my life inside. One by one, I carried them downstairs to my father's Buick.

As I stared at the last box, Beck's light footsteps were unusually audible in the stagnant silence. I turned around to face her for the last time—something I'd dreaded from the moment I realized we were actually breaking up. She held my hand loosely as I looked around the loft that was no longer *ours*. It seemed erroneous to leave such a beautiful place and say goodbye to such a lovely woman, but there was no other option. The chasm between us was irreparable. Beck's grip tightened slightly as tears threatened to detonate her composure. So I let my fingers slip slowly out of hers and shut the door softly behind me.

Chapter 24

London, September 1930

It was late September, and London's streets were every shade of gray. The city smelled of coal smoke, brackish water, and stale fog. I walked at a hurried pace until I noticed the billboard and stopped dead in my tracks. It was the only colorful thing in sight, with her face magnified to a breathtaking volume. Rouged lips, rosy cheeks, and those sparkling green eyes. She was the kind of beautiful that steals a bit of your soul whenever you see her.

It was the first time I'd been back to London in so many years. I tried to distract myself by looking at the antique dishes in local market's colorful stalls. Rustic saucers sat alongside vintage china and eclectic jewelry. It fascinated me how such different treasures could coexist together, side by side. I would normally spend hours getting lost in a place like that. Still, my mind was preoccupied with that giant billboard. I couldn't stop thinking about the woman on it. I guess I'd never really fallen out of love with her.

MY shaky hands could barely clasp the cappuccino sitting in front of me. I pulled out the sealed white envelope and strongly considered opening it, but I was too scared of the hypothetical message inside. *Why did my parents keep it all these years? Why didn't they ever give it to me?*

I saw Scarlett through the café window and immediately wondered why life turned out the way it did. I couldn't help but stare, tracing her red lips down to her long neck and svelte frame. She wore a white blouse tucked into a black ballerina skirt. Her long blond hair rustled in the wind as she noticed me, and my heart skipped a couple beats. She smiled and I smiled back, blushing at the sight of her after all those years.

As she walked in, the first thing I noticed was her unmistakable gaze. Her eyes were even greener than I remembered. Her skin was taut and devoid of wrinkles, especially around her eyes and mouth. I wondered how much she had actually smiled since Oxford.

Scarlett nodded at diners as she slowly walked by their tables. When she finally arrived at mine, she rested a familiar hand on my shoulder, sending chills down my spine.

"Amelia Cole," she whispered.

"Hello Scarlett," I managed to say.

She took the seat across from me and smoothed her skirt gracefully.

"Fame looks good on you," I muttered in an attempt to break the ice.

She just looked back at me with a curious expression. I wanted to know what she was thinking.

I cleared my throat. "So, how are you?" My nervous energy was exacerbated by the caffeine in my system.

"I'm really good," she said, smiling.

I wasn't sure if I believed her or not.

Her delicate fingers were accented with clusters of rose gold rings. But one in particular stood out. A princess-cut diamond on her left hand.

"*Scarlett.*" My stomach clenched. "You're married." I was asking and telling at the same time.

"Engaged," she whispered. "*James.* He's a good man."

"Do you love him?"

"In my own way, yes."

"Well, I'm happy for you both," I said without really meaning it.

"It's a little late in life, but better late than never, right?" A forced smile spread across her lips. "And you?"

"Oh no, I'm not married," I said quietly. "Never found anyone quite as interesting after I left England."

There was a glimmer in her eyes as the sentiment registered.

"Oh rubbish," Scarlett countered. "You're telling me that you've *never* been with anyone else in ten long years?"

Her playful tone reminded me of the girls we once were. But a shiny engagement ring told me otherwise.

"I just meant that I never married," I said quietly into my porcelain cup. The frothy milk had sunken into an inch of lukewarm coffee.

Scarlett raised a prying eyebrow, tempting me to tell her all about Beck. I wondered if I should catch her up on the tumultuous years since Oxford.

"I—" but something stopped me cold. Probably the realization that she would tell me all about her experiences during the past ten years as well . . . including James and other topics I didn't want to hear about. So I changed the subject.

"There *is* something I've been wanting to ask you though, Scarlett . . ."

"Ask away." She waved a slender hand through the thick café air.

"That conversation we had in London . . ."

Her shoulders stiffened, and I got the sense that she knew exactly what I was going to ask.

"The acting. Did you ever—?"

"Amelia. I never . . ." Her voice fell off, and she leaned closer. "*We* were never an act. I meant everything I said." She gripped the edge of the table. "The thing is . . . Will and I . . ."

"What about you and Will?"

She shook her head.

"The three of us had so much fun at Oxford," I ventured.

She nodded her head and gave a half smile.

"I heard that Wonderland burned down."

"Yes," she said quietly. "There was . . . a fire."

"I wonder—"

"To fully answer your question," she said, "my love for you was nothing but real. You were the only person I could ever let my guard down with."

And then we were both lost for words. Everyone around us was chatting, laughing, and sipping hot coffee, but Scarlett and I were frozen in silence.

Eventually, I had no choice but to break it. "Can't we at least be friends?"

My question hung in the espresso-scented air, waiting to be answered.

"I—I don't know how to be your friend, Amelia. I'm not sure I ever did."

"We were friends for a while at Oxford."

"No." She sighed. "It was always something more."

"We *were* friends," I insisted. "Before we . . . fell in love."

"But the two weren't ever really separate, were they?"

Now her question hung in front of me, and we both knew the answer. I didn't know what to say next, so I pulled out her letter and set it on the table between us.

"What is that?"

"An unopened letter from 1920, if you can believe it. I found it as I was rummaging through my parents' study this summer. They had it all this time."

"*You never opened it?*" Recognition flooded her face, and the rosy color drained from it.

"No," I answered.

"I was wondering why you called after all this time," she said. "I didn't even believe my agent when he told me."

"Well, I found this and I guess it conjured up a lot of memories . . . and feelings."

"You shouldn't read it," she said quietly. It doesn't really matter now . . ."

"Scarlett." I swallowed hard. "I never really stopped loving you."

"Nor I you," she said resolutely.

"I just wish—"

"You and I both realized that the world wouldn't accept what we wanted." She smiled faintly. "So we swore off stars."

"I didn't," I countered.

"You did, though," she said. "When you left."

I shook my head slowly. She was wrong.

"You gave up on us." She didn't say it sensitively or bitterly. She just said it.

"I never did," I insisted.

"I don't blame you though," she said, as if she hadn't heard me. "I didn't give you much hope, did I?"

I hated the thought that either of us swore off stars, that we renounced the possibility of *us*. I couldn't fathom it.

"I used to believe in stars," I breathed. "I believed in you and me."

"So did I, Lia," she said, her voice barely audible.

Our conversation came to an inconclusive end, and I walked out of the coffee house feeling more conflicted than I had before. Teary-eyed, I stuck the letter into my coat pocket and tried my best to forget. I didn't want to waste another minute thinking about the woman I couldn't be with.

PART II

Chapter 25

Brooklyn, September 1949

The war aged me more than time itself. When the United States first got involved in 1941, I thought about quitting my job at the paper. We faced a lot of turnover at the office after Pearl Harbor—the attacks left people terrified to even leave their homes, much less report from the field. I was seriously close to turning in my notice, but there were so many stories that needed to be told. So I stayed on the paper and continued my work during the war.

I spent most of my free time volunteering at the hospital, bandaging the physical wounds of young men. Most of them were nineteen or twenty, fresh out of their family homes. I'll never forget their dusty eyes—glazed over with an understanding that only war can bring.

I thought little about Scarlett because my thoughts were consumed with battlefield bruises and head injuries. But sometime after the chaos calmed, I started thinking of her again. I went back to work and sifted through my old reporting notebooks—covered in pencil observations I'd made when I still believed in love. Slowly and steadily, I began to remember the girl I used to be.

As I sat at my old desk one evening, my apartment felt especially barren. It was unused, untouched by anyone but me. I reached into a rusty top drawer, looking for a pack of chewing gum or some other distraction. What I found was much more than I expected: Scarlett's letter, postmarked Oxford–October, 1920.

For a while, all I could do was stare. I barely remembered stuffing the unopened envelope into a messy stack of papers and journals. Then again, nearly twenty years had passed since I'd shown her the letter. The world was a different place now.

Still in an odd limbo between cynicism and optimism, I turned the letter over in my trembling hands. Maybe I owed it to myself to open the wrinkled envelope. I couldn't deny that I was curious about what her writing would reveal. Maybe it would throw me back into another time, or maybe it would break my heart all over again.

I put on a pair of boots and walked up to the rooftop of my apartment building. A gentle breeze rustled the envelope's edges, daring me to open it. So I did.

Amelia,

I hope this finds you well in New York City. I apologize for not writing to you sooner . . . it's been quite an interesting year. I have great news—women can matriculate from Oxford as of next week! October 20th, to be exact. Can you believe it? A long, long journey, but WE DID IT! I'm sure you've heard all about the decision, but I wanted it to come from me also.

I have something else to tell you, Lia. I lied to you before you left. I acted like we weren't worth it, but in my heart I knew that we were. I was scared, but I should have fought harder for you ... for us.

If you can ever find it in your heart to forgive me, please write back. I know that I ruined everything and betrayed your trust. For that, I am eternally sorry. But I still love you, Lia. I want to be with you too. Come back to England and we'll run away together to any place you'd like. I PROMISE.

Forever Yours,
Scarlett

I stared at the paper in my hands, rereading that pivotal line.

we'll run away together to any place you'd like.

But it was too late. Nearly thirty years of life had rendered me a completely different person than the girl I'd been back then. I was less fragile and much surer of myself. As a single, forty-nine-year-old woman, I *had* to be. Of course I was still open to love, but I also felt okay on my own. I spent most of my time supporting political campaigns for women's rights. The fire Oxford sparked in me during college had never quite died out.

I paused for a moment and looked down at my brown boots. A tiny white paper was resting atop the worn leather. It must have fallen out of the envelope. I bent down to pick it up and quickly realized what it was. My heart stopped as *what-ifs* flashed through my head. I was holding a first-class boat ticket to England.

Come back to England and we'll run away together to anyplace you'd like.

The strength I'd built up ruptured immediately. Before I could even think about how expensive that ticket must have been, its sentiment took over. Tears flooded my tired eyes as I turned the ticket over in my fingers. I searched the corners of my mind for an answer. All I wanted was a reason why we would have been impossible. A justification for the separate lives we were living.

If there's one thing I know, it's that history repeats itself. I had always thought of Scarlett and me as different planets in the same orbit. We had collided once; maybe we would collide once more, creating a bright explosion of redemption and memories and broken promises. Maybe we'd get a second chance to make up for the first one we never really had. I closed my eyes and tried to imagine it. *Scarlett and me, together for real.* For a moment, it almost seemed possible. *We'd smile and laugh without regret. I'd kiss her shamelessly and love her boldly. Nothing would stop us.*

Before I got too lost in the hypothetical, I opened my eyes to take in Brooklyn's autumn air. It was dark and I knew that I should probably go back inside. But before I turned around, I did something that I'd forbidden myself to do years earlier. Ever so slowly, I raised my gaze up to the night sky. It was radiant, breathtaking, and everything at once. Tears ran down my face as I let myself stare at the brilliant stars once more.

THREE weeks had passed since I opened that emotional letter. I was still trying to figure out how to put it all behind me. *Why on earth did I have to find that letter in the first place?* I was simply organizing my parents' study, and there it was. I was sure they hadn't kept it from me on purpose. After all, they had no idea who Scarlett Daniels even was. It must have been an honest misplacement. Oddly enough, though, the letter almost seemed to find me.

I had tried to be amicable with her that day in the coffee shop. In my opinion, we had been great friends before it turned into something more. *But not according to Scarlett.* God, she was so stubborn sometimes. If she refused to at least be friendly, the situation was out of my hands. She was a married woman now.

I eventually resumed my routine and went back to work. The journal I wrote for—*Eastern Weekly,* a politically-driven paper with medium-sized circulation—had offices in both Brooklyn and Manhattan. I had recently been promoted to managing editor, which was still a shock to me, considering that some of the men in the office didn't think women should be working at all. Needless to say, I valued my job more than many things. I'd opted to work in Brooklyn, since it was a casual office environment and much closer to my apartment.

I'd become heavily involved with the National Women's Trade Union League after graduating college in the twenties, advocating for improved wages and working conditions for women. From there, I'd gone on to intern at a local paper, and had worked my way up to staff writer. I loved interviewing political figures and writing about current issues. It felt like I was making a contribution, even if it was a small one.

After women won the right to vote, I assumed equality would flourish. But that wasn't the case. Many were satisfied with the newfound suffrage, unmotivated to continue the fight. It appalled me. My passion for my work was one of the things that had ended my relationship with Beck.

Our office was male-dominated like any other, but I made an effort to involve as many women as possible in the journal's production, especially now that the war was over. Besides secretarial jobs, I had fought for the creation of other positions that benefitted from female employees. The paper had become more balanced in the many years I'd worked there, and now that I was managing editor, I hoped to effect even more change.

Work occupied most of my time, but I preferred it that way. I tried to see the few friends I'd managed to keep in my life on the weekends. I couldn't even remember the last time I'd seen Robbie. He enlisted in the military shortly after marrying Ness—something that she'd unsuccessfully tried to talk him out of. Robbie never quite moved on from his brother's death, and enlisting was his way of feeling closer to Ben. Robbie's marital rift resulted in a heartbreaking divorce—he left for the war, and Ness left him. Between our mutual romantic failures, everything had just sort of fallen apart.

My parents and I had continued to have a tumultuous relationship for many years. I was never quite content after coming home from Oxford, and I think they realized that early on. While I was cordial with Beck, we hardly talked anymore. Moving in with my parents after our breakup had its challenges, but I didn't have any other options at the time. They never found out about our long-term relationship, and I was happy to keep them in the dark. These days we were spending a lot of time together, and even getting along well now that they were much older. I cooked dinner for them at the restaurant every other Sunday. They never *did* open another location like Robbie predicted they would. I think that money had always just been a little too tight.

I arrived for an overdue visit on a particularly warm fall evening.

"Lia." My mother hugged me tightly. "You're late!"

"Sorry Mom." I sighed. "Another busy day at the journal."

"It's the weekend, honey! You shouldn't even be working."

"I'm researching a new piece about women's wages. It's—"

"Please, Lia. It's Sunday . . ."

She flashed me a concerned expression.

"Sorry, but you know I love my work."

"Maybe that's the problem," she said under her breath, just loud enough for me to hear.

"*Mom?*"

"You know how I feel, sweetheart. You should be married to a nice man and have grown children of your own by now. But instead you're spending hours *working* in an office!"

"I'm making a difference at the paper," I said firmly.

We'd had this frustrating conversation many times over the years.

"At least you had the chance to meet men when you were living in the city—"

"I moved there for *school*, Mom. Then I tried to focus on my job, remember?"

"Well," she signed. "Maybe you shouldn't have—"

"Let's not talk about that tonight, eh Mary?"

My dad walked in right on cue. "How are ya, sweetie?" He planted a sloppy kiss on my forehead.

"Good, thanks, Dad." I smiled.

My mom rolled her eyes and muttered something else before returning to the kitchen. I heard an unnecessary clattering of pots and pans until she calmed down.

"So why haven't we seen ya in so long, huh, Lia?"

"It's only been a few weeks," I said, chuckling.

"Much too long." My dad shook his head and grinned.

"I—I've been a little preoccupied."

"With work?"

"Sort of . . ."

"C'mon, Lia. What's been going on?"

"An old letter, actually. From a very old friend."

"Which old friend?" He looked genuinely confused.

"You don't know her. Just someone from Oxford."

He gave me a curious look.

"I found it in your study a long time ago . . ."

I heard a porcelain dish hit the floor.

"You okay?" I called to my mom.

There was no reply, and I started walking toward the kitchen.

I felt my dad's firm grip on my shoulder. "Let's just leave her be, darlin'."

He led me into the restaurant's banquet room, and we sat down at one of the rustic wooden tables. I fiddled with my navy tea dress as he stared strangely at me.

"What's wrong?" I asked quietly.

But he didn't answer. Instead, my father ran his fingers across the flawed wood in front of him.

"*Dad?*"

The delectable smell of fresh pasta drifted in from the kitchen. Mom was making her specialty, *Orecchiette a la Lia*. I used to help her in the kitchen when I was younger, usually resulting in catastrophe. This dish was one of our few successes, so she'd named it after me. She loved telling customers the story of how I kept throwing chilies into her saucepan until the entire kitchen smelled of nose-tingling spice. Just smelling it now, I could taste the simmering sauce and feel its peppery flavors dance around my mouth. My head turned toward the kitchen, anticipating the scrumptious dinner ahead of us.

"I know about Scarlett," my dad said faintly.

It was enough to send me reeling around in my chair. I looked at my dad's weathered face, searching for a slight grin or twinkle in his eye. But there was nothing. I knew that he was serious.

"What do you mean?" I ventured, trying to hide my surprise.

"Lia, I *know*," he said again.

"But—how?" I didn't understand how this was possible.

"I read the letter all those years ago."

"What?" I couldn't comprehend what he was saying. "But it was sealed."

"And then I noticed that the letter was gone," he said. "My fault for not moving it before you organized our study."

"Dad . . . I don't—"

"I guess it slipped my mind." He shrugged. "Thirty years is a long time . . ."

"Dad!"

I felt like he was ignoring me.

"I felt bad for reading it, hun. That's why I resealed it. I wanted to throw it away—I really did. But I just felt too damn guilty each time."

"Why would you—"

"We thought you seemed different after coming back from Oxford. You were *withdrawn* . . ."

"But why would you be suspicious of a letter?"

My dad looked down, avoiding my inquisitive eyes.

"We just—"

"Tell me," I said firmly.

He stared down again until the tension was intolerable.

"Robbie."

His name in this context made me feel sick. My stomach tightened, as a lump grew in my throat.

"He wanted to help you."

"Help me?" I felt betrayed. *Betrayed by Robbie and deceived by my parents.*

"Lia—"

"Don't," I said loudly.

"Honey, you have to understand—"

"Understand *what?* That you ruined my chances of ever being satisfied with this life?" I was fuming now. "You have no idea what you did!"

"We were trying to protect you!" It was the first time I'd heard my dad yell in years.

"How could you read that letter and not even *tell* me about it?"

He just stared at me, eyes watery underneath his furrowed brow.

My mother walked in with a platter of fresh pasta. "Amelia—"

"You knew?" I hissed.

She looked at the floor and said nothing.

"I was depressed for an entire year after I came back," I cried.

"We just didn't want—"

"I don't want to see either of you for a long, *long* time."

I felt like a moody teenager again—fighting with my parents over something important that they deemed trivial. I couldn't form another coherent thought. I stormed out of the restaurant as they called after me, with no intention of ever going back.

Chapter 26

SCARLETT

replay that day in my head. It's been almost twenty years, but I still feel like I'm there: *1930, London—before the war.* I walk into the coffee shop and there she is, lovely like always. But it was never physical beauty that drew me to her. It was the way she looked at me . . . what she saw in me . . . what she made me see in myself. Her confidence, intelligence, and unwavering belief in us.

I walk coolly by each table and give the obligatory smile here and there. It's just part of being under the public eye. She looks nervous, uncomfortable even. I wonder if she senses my anxiety, despite my best attempt to mask it.

Of course she notices the ring. I have to wear it in public—James would be beside himself if the photographers caught even a glimpse of my bare hand. Her face falls as I tell her about him. I want to explain everything, but it's not the right time or place.

And that letter. I nearly pass out when she sets it on the table. I stare at her and she stares back at me with that same piercing gaze she's always had. *Why is it still unopened?* I don't understand.

Then Amelia tells me that her parents had the letter from all those years ago. That she accidentally found it in a cluttered desk in their study. *That she never even had a chance to read it.* It's too much to swallow.

It's not that I don't want to see her again. On the contrary, I've wanted to see her for so bloody long. I've wanted to be with her every second of every day. But there's so much more to consider now. There's James and my neurotic agent, Joe, to worry about. I can only imagine what they'd do if they found out about Lia and me. Not to mention everyone else who might try to bring us down.

Chapter 27

LIA

I was trapped beneath a pile of emotional rubble, struggling to breathe. A mixture of rage and confusion coursed through my body as I tried to forget again. I tried to eject the past three decades from my memory banks. But it was *impossible*. Scarlett Daniels had left an indelible imprint on my heart.

I threw myself into work even harder than usual. Some nights were spent at the office, devoid of sleep and full of strong coffee. As each of my coworkers left for the evening, they exchanged concerned looks of pity and confusion. I briefly wondered what it would be like to have someone to go home to. *How would that feel?* I tried to shake off every unproductive thought and bury myself in stories and edits.

My chatty secretary, Giselle, eventually forced me out of the office.

"You have to at least go home and shower," she said with an upturned nose one morning. "And put on some fresh clothes."

I agreed reluctantly. "But I'll be back later this afternoon," I said as she shooed me out of the office.

The spotty sun quickly faded during my walk home, and I found myself caught in an East Coast rainstorm without an umbrella. The angry sky glared down at me behind a thick layer of clouds. I tried to hail a taxi but quickly realized they were all taken. Water sloshed around in my boots as I hurried home. The walk home to my tiny apartment took thirty minutes.

As I approached the depressing beige building I called home, a rain-soaked man caught my attention. My father was sitting on the worn-down front step. I almost dropped my chunky keychain before curbing my surprise.

"You shouldn't be here," I said.

"We've been calling you every day," he countered.

"Well, I've been busy."

My dad shot me a frustrated look.

"Please, *please* let me tell you the whole story," he pleaded.

I shook my head and walked past him, approaching the tall iron gates in front of my apartment complex. My icy hands trembled, and I failed to place the correct key in the simple lock. Between the rainwater running down my face and tears creeping out of my tired eyes, I was a mess.

I felt my father behind me. "Please, Lia, my love." He placed his hands lightly on top of mine, and we unlocked the gates together.

We walked slowly and silently up the six flights of stairs to my unit. He remained five paces behind me the entire time. I left the door open after I stepped inside, but didn't say a word to my dad. Instead I lay down on my fluffy sofa, sopping wet and quivering from the cold.

I must have drifted off from exhaustion, because a crackling fire woke me up some time later. Orange and amber tones illuminated my normally dim apartment. I turned over, warm despite the damp sofa cushions beneath me, and realized that my dad must have covered me with a blanket while I slept. I blinked twice and he came into focus, sitting calmly in a leather armchair across the room. He smiled at me sadly, and then spoke softly.

"I'm going to explain, okay?"

I stared at him with the same confused hostility I'd felt during our last encounter. "I can't talk to you right now," I said flatly.

"I'm serious."

"Look, I don't know what *Robbie* told you, but—"

"Lia. He was trying to help."

"What on earth did he say? Robbie doesn't even know the whole story." I mentally acknowledged the lie as it left my lips.

"He told me that there was someone at Oxford . . . a female student . . ."

I couldn't help but feel sorry for my poor, conservative dad, struggling to put it all into words.

"He told you that I was . . . *homosexual?*" I asked quietly.

He stared out into the darkness and nodded. "I think that he still loved you and was worried about you . . ."

"I haven't seen Robbie in ages," I said sourly.

My dad continued to stare out the apartment window, looking for something that wasn't there.

"I *am*," I said softly. "*Homosexual*, I mean."

He broke his stare and slowly turned back toward me. "I know, sweetie. I know."

I tried to think of something to say next, but couldn't. So my father filled the void.

"Robbie came to me because he was concerned. Not about you being *homosexual*, but about what could happen to you if"— his sturdy voice broke—"He wanted us to know the truth . . . said you were worried about what we'd think."

I nodded slightly.

"This was just a few months after you returned home. Your mother and I were sure that he was mistaken. But then that letter came and . . ."

"You were scared that he was right." I said what he couldn't.

He nodded again.

"And Mom?"

"She was more terrified than I was. We'd heard so many stories over the years about people being attacked and injured—or worse. The thought of you being institutionalized or becoming one of those tragedies . . ."

"Why didn't you ever talk to me about it?"

"We didn't know what to say, my love. I still don't."

"I'm still your daughter, Dad," I whispered. "I'm still *me*."

"I know that, baby," he said. He stood up and walked over to me.

"So many years . . ." I shook my head. "And you thought that hiding the letter would—"

"I'm sorry," he murmured as tears welled beneath his wrinkly eyelids. "I'm so sorry, Lia."

We talked for the rest of the night. There was more yelling and screaming and crying. There was frustration and resentment and regret. But in the end, there was understanding.

※

I awoke with newfound strength and a welcome sense of ease. I crept out of my bedroom and saw my dad sleeping on the sofa. He was snoring softly, and his quiet breath made me beam for the first time in a while. I walked into the kitchen, noticing how the early-morning light flattered its bright cherry-red walls and overused appliances. I ran my fingers along the white enamel oven and sighed—I'd cooked so many meals for one on that stovetop. As fragrant coffee brewed, I thought back to my last conversation with Scarlett. *Why did it end so abruptly?*

"So what do we do now?"

"The same thing we've been doing for the past ten years," she said.

"But Scarlett, we've finally found a way back to each other . . ."

"Happy accident," she muttered, tilting her head to the side.

"You don't even want me back in your life?" I asked, growing desperate.

"I wish that you could have been in my life for the past decade. But things change, Lia."

What did she mean? *That wasn't the Scarlett that I used to know and love. She was so composed, so devoid of every emotion I couldn't seem to suppress. There I was, tearing my heart out and handing it to her—laying my soul right on the table—and all she could do was look away and flash her million-dollar smile in the other direction. I realized that nothing was going to change. So I got up and walked out.*

"Good morning, darlin'." My dad startled me out of my trance.

"Oh—good morning."

"You okay?" He put his callused hand on my shoulder and gave me a quick peck on the cheek.

"Coffee's ready," I murmured, realizing that our conversation would take several nights to fully sleep off.

"Cream and sugar?"

I nodded and walked over to the sturdy table Robbie had handcrafted for me several years earlier. Coffee rings caught my attention as I ran my hand over its smooth surface. After pulling out one of the mahogany chairs, I looked around my cozy apartment. The living room was filled with a strange energy from the night before. I didn't know exactly how to feel.

"Here ya go, hun." My dad put two mugs of steamy joe on the table and sat down.

"Thanks, Dad."

I took a long sip of burning hot coffee and looked out the window. Another overcast day with clouds proliferating in the sky.

"You have to go after her, Lia."

I let the words drift around me for a while before responding. "I only told you about all that because I wanted to be honest. But what's done is done, Dad. I'm an old woman now."

"And what does that make me?"

"A slightly *older* man." I smiled.

My dad shook his head and laughed. My parents had me when they were only sixteen.

"The way you talk about Scarlett . . . I can tell you still love her."

"Why are you suddenly so supportive of me?"

"I've always supported you, Lia. But this . . . *this* was hard to accept. I'm sorry that it took me so long. But I'm here for you now like I couldn't be back then."

"It's okay, Dad. I've moved on."

"Sweetie, you've done incredible things for others. I admire all of the measures you fight for. I really do. But I know that work has become your entire life—"

"It gives me purpose."

"And that's great. But you can't give up on love, honey. Especially a love like this."

I looked into his twinkling eyes and wondered what our conversation would have been like several years earlier. *Would we even be talking? Would my parents have tried to understand then as he's trying to now?*

After I hugged my father good-bye, I thought about what he said. My love for Scarlett had endured heartbreak and time, doubt and rejection. Was it still worth fighting for?

Chapter 28

I spent a whole month trying to answer that very question. Some days made me feel like our love *was* worth fighting for, while others convinced me that it was not. Scarlett had made no attempt to contact me after our meeting in London nineteen years before, which I took as a discouraging sign, to say the least. Then again, her lost letter more than spoke for itself.

I reread it by the fire one night when I couldn't sleep. Her words leaped off the page and into my head as I replayed everything over and over again. I turned the wrinkled paper over in my hands, much as I had done with Scarlett's coral ribbon on that first fateful day we met.

Perhaps it was that lingering memory, or maybe it was something else. But the next morning left me feeling optimistic and determined. I resolved to go after Scarlett Daniels one more time. If it didn't work, I would accept the failure as permanent defeat. But I had to try to win her back for one last time before giving up on us completely.

I fished her old agent's business card out of my cluttered desk drawer and stared at his telephone number. I wasn't even sure if they were still working together. My fingers hovered over the phone for a full minute before I worked up the courage to dial.

A gruff voice finally answered on the tenth ring.

"Joe Lancaster speaking. Who's this?"

"Mr. Lancaster, hello. This is Amelia Cole, calling about Scarlett?"

"*Who?*"

"Her good friend from Oxford?"

There was no response.

"Never mind," I sighed. "I was wondering if you might be able to connect me with Scarlett. We used to be . . . great friends."

"I don't give out Ms. Daniels' personal number. If you're some kind of press—"

"I'm not a journalist, Mr. Lancaster," I lied.

"Look, whoever you are, don't call this number again. Ms. Daniels is a very busy woman and I'm an even busier man!"

I hung up the receiver and looked out into Brooklyn's dismal Tuesday sky. *What a frustrating conversation.* It was a wonder I'd ever gotten through to him years ago. *Now what?*

Between appointments and work consultations, I devoted my time to searching out Scarlett's whereabouts—secretly, of course. Although my coworkers knew a lot about me, nobody at the journal was privy to the details of my past. The news staff was intelligent and forward-thinking, but that didn't mean they wouldn't talk outside of the office. I couldn't take any chances.

After another busy week, I had done absolutely nothing but burn myself out. Scarlett was nowhere to be found, and her staff members were being extremely discreet about her current filming schedule. Her hair stylist, Collette, hung up on me mid-sentence before I could ask where she was. And her publicist, Nathan, never returned my calls—his secretary blatantly asked me to stop calling after my fourth attempt.

I crawled into bed with the intention of reading *The House of Mirth*, but drifted off into sleep instead.

"Lia," she whispers.

"Hmm?"

"Wake up, sleepyhead. It's Christmas!"

"Too early," I murmur as I pull the fluffy white duvet over my head. "More sleep . . ."

"We have to go explore London," Scarlett says, rubbing my back softly.

I move slowly out of my sleepy haze. "Christmas?" I ask, finally opening my eyes to look at her.

Scarlett nods and smiles down at me from the feathery hotel pillow she's perched on, loose blond curls tumbling over her bare shoulders.

"Let's stay here forever," I whisper as I pull her back into bed with me.

Something glass shattered in the apartment above mine. I opened my eyes, startled but still impossibly drowsy. A bitter draft rushed in from my open window, but I was too tired to get up and close it. The chills sent me further underneath my covers, hiding from the Brooklyn cold and the hectic day ahead of me. I lay there for another hour, caught somewhere in between awareness and slumber. The warm scene from my dream washed over me, and then another unwelcome breeze chased it away, confirming that it was just that, a memory.

Without an umbrella or decent hat, I stepped out of my apartment building and into the rain. Drops fell onto my lashes, and I continuously brushed them away. As bright yellow taxis drove by, I crossed the muddy path that I took almost every day. *Left, right, left . . .*

"Lia?"

My head whirled around before I could process the sound.

"I thought it was you."

Robbie Wells stood directly in front of me.

My jaw dropped open. *"Robbie."* I could barely believe it.

We stood there, stationary, as hurried cars drove by and heavy showers soaked our heads.

※

FIVE emotionally charged hours later, and I felt back to normal with Robbie Wells. The conversation started off all wrong; we kept talking over each other in between long, dramatic pauses. But about an hour into our long-overdue exchange, something changed.

"What happened to you?" I gestured to the thick scar on his right arm.

"Bullet wound," he said matter-of-factly.

"That's awful."

"It's not so bad. I did what I could over there, you know." Robbie stared out my window as sheets of rain pelted the glass.

"Are you discharged, then?"

"Not yet, but hopefully soon." His gray eyes were remote as he continued. "Fifteen-plus years, I served . . ."

"That's a long time."

"I did things, Lia. *Horrible* things." His remorseful tone scared me.

"It was a war, Robbie," I whispered.

"Yes," he said quietly.

Robbie was lost in a memory—something I could identify because I knew the feeling. Silence plagued my cold apartment until he spoke again.

"So . . . you're still working for the paper, then?" He set his mug on my oak coffee table.

"Yes. I volunteered as a nurse for a while, though . . ."

"Oh?"

"I'd be at the office during the day, then go to the hospital after work and on the weekends."

"Always keeping busy," he chuckled.

"It felt like the right thing," I responded. "Plus, I like keeping busy."

Robbie smiled.

"Any progress at work?"

"With the journal? I like to think that we make progress every day, but no monumental strides. We haven't had a real breakthrough in a while . . ."

"*I'm sorry*, Lia."

"It's okay. I mean, it's odd going to work every day when you—"

"I mean about telling your dad."

"Oh." I wasn't prepared to launch into that discussion again. I didn't even realize that my dad had contacted Robbie.

"Really, I am."

"Okay," I said quietly.

"I was just trying to help—"

"Yeah, I know. Because you thought that you knew best, right?"

"No. Because I loved you."

"Robbie, I—"

"Oh, c'mon. I told you that years ago."

"I remember . . ."

"That time we spent together changed my life," he said.

"Me too, but in a very different way—"

"I know." His mouth twisted in a wry smile as he placed his hand on top of mine.

"I'm sorry too," I said. "For telling you about everything when you came to visit. I can only imagine how hard—"

"Don't be," he whispered.

"Do you want to talk about it?"

"Oh, Lia. It's in the past."

It was strange to realize that Robbie and I had never talked about that day at Oxford. Not even after I lived with him in New York.

"But you never even said anything to me after that day I told you about Scarlett," I objected. "You went off to London for a holiday and we didn't see each other again until I was back home."

"Didn't have to say anything." He shook his head.

"What do you mean?"

"When I saw you that day at Oxford, you were different. I'd never seen you so happy."

I looked down at my lap.

"And when you see the girl you love so blissfully unaware,"

he said, "you don't want to ruin that for her. Besides, you explained everything to me."

"It was that simple for you?"

"It was hard at first, but I carried on as best I could. And so much has happened since then. I ended up meeting Ness, and . . . the rest is history." He forced a smile.

"You *loved* her like no one else," I said quietly.

"I did," Robbie agreed. "I do."

"Do you ever see her?" I asked hesitantly.

"No." He shook his head. "An old mutual friend updates me sometimes."

I nodded.

"She's remarried with kids now," he said quietly. "A completely different person, I imagine."

"I'm sorry, Robbie."

"Don't be . . . I've moved on the best I could. Not sure you have, though. From Scarlett, I mean."

We sat still, finally on the same page after so many years.

"You have to go after her," he urged.

"You sound exactly like my father," I said, laughing.

"I'm serious. Even after Beck and everything else, it was always Scarlett."

"I don't even know where she is, Robbie."

He looked at me and grinned.

"What?"

"I do."

"You're kidding."

"Nope."

"Robbie."

He smiled and took a long sip of his coffee. "My friend John Miller knows her publicist. And he sort of bribed her to reveal Scarlett's next movie location."

"He didn't."

"He did."

"I don't believe that . . ."

"Believe it, Lia. And they're shooting in Hong Kong, of all places."

"Hong Kong?"

"Yep. Asian city with expensive silk and spicy food. Ever heard of it?" He winked.

"You're funny," I said sarcastically.

"Well," he put his finger to his lips. "I guess it's technically a British colony again . . ."

"Isn't it both?"

"Probably," Robbie sighed. "I don't know."

He shrugged casually.

"Here, John wrote down the set location," he said, handing me a paper café napkin.

I stared at the numbers scribbled on the napkin then looked back at Robbie.

"Thank you," I whispered. "*Thank you.*"

"Don't mention it," he smiled.

I grinned back as an intriguing thought crossed my mind.

"We didn't just *accidentally* bump into each other this morning, did we?"

Robbie just smiled harder.

We both stood up on my matted wool rug, still damp from our wet shoes. I stretched out my arms and gave him a giant hug. As we held each other, I savored the fact that I didn't blame him for anything or feel guilty about what happened. It was just nice to have my friend back.

Chapter 29

Hong Kong, November 1949

SCARLETT

"Come to bed," he begs.

"Soon," I say as I pat lotus blossom cream onto my décolletage.

"Please."

"I will, James."

He's propped up on our luxury hotel bed, shirtless and staring at me. I rearrange lotions and perfume bottles on the vanity, struggling to come up with yet another excuse to stay where I am.

"Baby," he says, standing up. "I haven't had you in months." I watch him through the mirror, sauntering over until he's standing behind me. "You really know how to torture a man." He grins.

I force a laugh and turn back to the vanity.

"I want you," he whispers into my right ear.

I feel him harden as he circles my waist, gently tugging on my silk chemise.

"Please."

I let him draw me up and lead me to the bed. Sex with a man isn't bad once you know what to expect. I've done it before and I'm sure I'll do it again. Compulsory maintenance, I guess. I sort of shut off and go somewhere else for a bit. I used to think of Lia, but that's impossible now.

"That was great," he murmurs afterward.

I sit up and he lays his heavy head on my left thigh. Unsatisfied, I light a cigarette—a rare treat for me—and pass one to James. We each inhale simultaneously and blow out clouds of gray smoke.

I think about how he's basically been exploiting me for my fame. Our engagement resulted in a faux-marriage years ago—though we didn't actually love each other. While we're *man and wife* on paper, my heart will never belong to James. I'm sure he realizes by now that the attraction is far from mutual, but I do my best to stroke his ego every now and then. Despite my indifference, James knows that he's still a catch to the rest of the world . . . he's younger than me, good-looking, and well-established. He's all of those things and more, which is beneficial to *both* of our careers. The world still thinks of us as film industry sweethearts, but our reality is much different. James is using me. *That's the truth.* Then again, I'm using him too.

Chapter 30

LIA

Trunk in tow, I hailed a cab in the East Coast darkness.

"Airport, please," I said as the knot in my stomach tightened.

The ride felt longer than it probably was. I tried to suppress my hesitation and resist the urge to shout, *Turn around!* Doubts multiplied inside my head as we approached the airport. *What will Scarlett say? What if she's happily married with children? Will she reject me again?* The taxi pulled up to a large terminal, and the driver waited patiently as I fiddled with my wallet to locate the fare.

"Good luck," he said as he handed me my oversized trunk.

We hadn't spoken at all during the ride, but I'm sure he could tell that I was nervous about something.

"Thanks," I called back as I dragged my trunk over the curb.

It was my first time in an airport. I'd never had a reason to fly, especially since my fear of heights pretty much ruled it out. Sailing from New York to England had been bad enough, with the seasickness and sleepless nights. But this was a new challenge altogether.

Walking through the large terminal only amplified my fear. Anxious travelers buzzed around me as they talked about the thrills of flight. "I've done it twice before," one woman bragged. "Your first trip is always the hardest." I kept telling myself that I *had* to do this, that there was no other way. I could continue to live without Scarlett, or I could be brave and go to Hong Kong. In my mind, the latter was my only option.

I rummaged through my purse and pulled out the express visa Robbie had helped me acquire just days earlier—I still couldn't wrap my head around all the strings he'd pulled. I clutched it tightly while making my way to the security check-point. Most people were walking straight through without any problems or a show of ID—I let out a quick sigh of relief. I went to put my unnecessary visa away when the middle-aged man in front of me turned around.

"Where are you headed?" he asked behind a pair of smudged lenses.

"Hong Kong," I answered, surprised.

He nodded as I put my visa away.

"And you?"

"Los Angeles. I'm going to visit a friend there."

"Great," I smiled and closed my purse.

"Why are you flying to Hong Kong?"

He sounded suspicious to me, though it may have just been my paranoia.

"Just out of curiosity," I shrugged. The lie left my mouth before I could answer truthfully.

"Oh?"

"Yes. I've always wanted to see Hong Kong."

"Why is that?"

"It's supposed to be quite interesting," I answered, wondering why he was asking so many questions.

He cocked his head.

"Are you travelling alone?"

"I am," I said bluntly.

"No husband with you?"

I shook my head.

"No . . . *son* to accompany you?"

"Nope. Just me," I said proudly.

"What do you do?"

"Um—" I glanced past him to see why the line wasn't moving.

"I'm a journalist."

"A *journalist*?" He looked me up and down. "Not a lot of . . ."

"Female journalists?" I gave him a blank stare.

"Well, I mean . . ."

"Yes, Mr.—?"

"*Crowley*. Thomas Crowley," he clarified quickly.

"Yes, Mr. Crowley. The field is quite oversaturated with men, just as most fields are. Don't you think?"

"Women are—I mean, they should probably, you know . . ." He swallowed hard, unable to compose a decent response.

"The line is moving, Mr. Crowley."

He looked confused as I gestured ahead.

"Oh, right." He turned around quickly.

"Good luck in Los Angeles," I said under my breath.

For the first time in a while, I missed Will. Besides Robbie and my father, he was one of the few men I knew who supported women's rights. I knew there were more of them out there, but it seemed like my life revolved around traditionalists—even men at the paper were still resistant to their female co-workers. It was odd to think about my youthful mindset at Oxford. Back then, I had assumed that things would be different by the time I was older. In a way, they were. But in a different way, there was still so much further to go. I guess that's how the future always works, though—it's rarely as bright as you imagine it to be.

※

I looked around as I waited to board the aircraft. I was the only single female traveler in sight. There were a few young couples and some large families. A small group of businessmen stood near the window, looking restless. Two of them sipped coffee, while the other one fiddled with his briefcase. I watched as he stuffed a stack of papers inside the black leather case and then snapped it shut. An unmistakable logo covered its exterior—a large, golden "M." It stood for Mosaic, Scarlett's film company. *These men must be headed to her film set in Hong Kong!*

I stared at the briefcase, unable to believe my luck. I snapped out of it when a short announcement informed us that we would begin boarding the aircraft soon. I gathered up my things with a smile. It was almost too easy. I knew how I was going to find Scarlett now.

I watched the businessmen hand over their boarding passes and walk towards the plane. Their tailored suits disappeared quickly down the ramp. My anxiety grew as I waited for the line to move. Finally, I approached the aircraft with a slew of remaining passengers trailing behind.

No sooner had I stepped into the cabin than a chirpy stewardess greeted me with a postcard. "Hello, ma'am. Which row are you seated in?"

"Row twenty," I said with a smile and stuck the card into my purse.

"That's towards the *back* of the plane," she said, gesturing down the aisle.

"Thanks," I said under my breath.

After taking off my coat, I took my seat and fastened the blue lap belt tightly.

"Are you sure this is safe?" a man with a thick New York accent across the aisle from me asked.

"It's perfectly safe, sir," a younger stewardess said calmly.

She wore a fitted blue uniform and black patent leather Mary Janes. Her tiny pillbox hat sat atop a head of silky auburn hair. The shiny silver wings pinned to her chest sparkled under the cabin light.

"I don't know," the man said. He was middle-aged and portly, wearing thin-framed metal reading lenses. "My cousin said it's scary once you're up there—"

"We have medicine if you start to feel ill," the stewardess reassured him. "But I'm sure you'll be just fine."

Her pleasant tone seemed to soothe him for the time being. I briefly wondered why this man was flying in the first place, but that thought was quickly chased away by my fears about this trip. The thought of flying to a new country to find Scarlett, who might not even want to see me, was almost too much to stomach. I could hear my own heartbeat as I watched more passengers hurry onto the plane. A nicely-dressed woman and her son sat down a few rows in front of me. They seemed excited about the trip, putting me temporarily at ease. I pulled out the postcard the stewardess had handed me and stared at a black and white picture of a large plane—I wondered if it was the model I was sitting on. I thought about writing to Robbie to distract myself, but my hand was shaking too much to form proper letters. I smiled at the thought of him trying to read my illegible message.

I shut my eyes tightly; sleeping through the next several hours was my best strategy. Our pilot made a weather announcement as we started to taxi, but I struggled to follow along. My heavy eyelids started to close before we even made it to the runway.

I hear her blissful laugh. She's standing next to me, trying on a flamboyant holiday hat. I gaze at her reflection in the mirror in front of us and start to giggle. "You're too much."

"Well. I think I look . . . wonderful," Scarlett says, trying to keep a straight face. She fails, and collapses into laughter. "You try one on then!"

I study the array of festive accessories displayed around us. "You pick one for me."

"How about . . . this one," Scarlett mutters as she places a heavy bonnet on my head.

"I look like one of Santa's kitschy elves," I say, curtsying.

"Harrods's simply can't handle us," she declares with a fake sneer.

We both burst out laughing as the saleswoman flashes us a threatening look.

Suddenly I was thrown out of the store and back into the 1940s. I gripped the armrests with clammy palms as the plane jolted from side to side. Loud vibrations left me feeling more unsettled while my tensed fingers turned white. As the cabin came back into focus, I turned slightly and noticed an elderly woman staring in my direction and smiling.

"You were dreaming of something happy," she said, just loud enough for me to hear.

"Yes—yes I was," I said, taken aback.

"I could tell," she beamed.

I gave her a quick smile and turned back toward the window. As I stared into the morning sky, all I wanted was to keep dreaming about Scarlett Daniels. But more than that, I wanted to go back in time to that idyllic Christmas Day in 1919.

Chapter 31

Hong Kong, November 1949

After a few more days of turbulent flights, I was standing at my final destination. We had been heavily delayed because of "severe weather conditions," but it was only late afternoon in Hong Kong. All of the passengers walked off the plane slowly, tired from our long trip over.

As our flight crew guided us to the arrivals terminal, I stole my first glimpses of the British colony. Sunshine crept in through open windows and large doors. The airport felt rough and unfinished, like a construction zone. The building was humid and sweltering hot, and I immediately missed the frigid aircraft cabin. My skin was sticky with sweat, in desperate need of a good hotel shower.

I walked quickly to catch up with the group of first-class businessmen. The golden "M" was my north star. I couldn't afford to lose it.

The airport's customs area was overwhelming. I was ushered into a line leading to a set of intimidating counters with armed officials. I looked around for the businessmen, but they were being led to a much shorter line. I struggled to come up with a decent plan. They were definitely going to clear customs well before me, so I had no choice but to hope I'd see them outside. If worse came to worst, I would take a taxi to my hotel and figure everything out. I knew I would breathe easier after I made it to the other side.

"Next," a loud voice startled me.

I stepped up to a counter and handed over my passport.

"Cole?"

"Yes, Amelia Jane Cole," I said nervously.

The man looked down and said something inaudible. He handed back my passport stiffly. "Welcome to Hong Kong."

A wave of muggy air enveloped me as I stepped outside. Just as I'd suspected would be the case, the businessmen were nowhere to be seen. My shoulders dropped as I ambled over to the short taxi line.

⁕

THE Eastern Blossom Hotel was a long way from the airport. I dozed off in the backseat before arriving a while later. A hard stop jolted me awake as we pulled into a grand entrance. Lofty and palatial, the building loomed over me as I carried my trunk up to its double doors.

I'd only stayed in a few hotels before, but the opulent Blossom blew both of them out of the water. A lively doorman greeted me and took my luggage to a nicely dressed bellhop. I was escorted to my room upon check-in and given a pass to the Blossom's swimming pool. It was Olympic-sized, overflowing with chlorinated aqua water and surrounded by cushy teak lounge chairs. A polished glass ceiling revealed the sun-drenched sky above.

A Hollywood-style vanity and handmade lavender soaps were just some of the lovely amenities inside my room. I sat on my bed's fluffy down comforter and sighed, wishing that Scarlett was there with me. *What would my college-aged self say if she saw me now?*

I spent the rest of the afternoon sipping tea and reading old books in the hotel library. After a full night's sleep and another day's rest, I was ready to explore. I asked the hotel manager for recommendations, and he pointed me in the direction of a popular bazaar.

I wandered aimlessly through the dusty marketplace, wondering what I was really doing in Hong Kong. Once again, I found myself on the other side of the world without a solid plan. This city couldn't be farther from home, figuratively and factually. It pulsed with effervescent culture, shady business deals, and suppressed political uprising. If New York was a sophisticated young woman, Hong Kong was her fiery cousin.

The peppery scent of fresh spices infiltrated my nose as I took in my surroundings. The rows of exotic goods in the bazaar reminded me vaguely of London's flea markets. From gold watches to woodcarvings, blooming flowers to handmade trinkets, I had never seen so many treasures packed into one place.

I continued walking and noticed a woman bargaining for silk at a textile stall ahead.

"*Tài guile!*" she said firmly.

"You drive a hard bargain, miss," the owner replied in accented English.

The woman laughed and said something else in what I assumed to be Cantonese.

"*Hye*," the owner agreed as he flashed a toothless grin.

He accepted the coin money and shook her delicate hand. The woman stuffed the smooth silk into her oversized magenta handbag and nodded good-bye. Before she disappeared into the vivid market stalls, I saw her adjust the navy hat on her head and quickly reapply some rouge. *I would know those lips anywhere.* Scarlett.

I wanted to go after her. I wanted to surprise her and eloquently win her back. I wanted to recite the speech I'd strung together on the long flight over, as I soared above places I had never even dreamed about visiting. I wanted to impress her and make her fall back in love with me. Instead, I stood there and watched her walk away.

Red and green rickshaws raced past me when I left the market. I wandered slowly as fleeting thoughts and regrets bounced around my head. Hong Kong was still recovering from the war, and large numbers of Chinese refugees were pouring into the colony on a regular basis. As I passed by a corner ginger factory, I peered into its open windows. Rows of overworked employees moved in unison, hunching from exhaustion and sweating from the brutal heat. I continued to stare until a tall worker noticed me—there was nothing but fatigue in his shadowy eyes. I smiled and nodded at him, embarrassed that he saw me looking in the first place. He tilted his head slightly before returning my smile and going back to work.

Dirty paths turned into paved streets as I made my way

down to the harbor's blue waters. Craft stalls became expensive shops and storefronts. The lingering scent of pricey cologne replaced the muddled aroma of orchids and salted meat. The sight was lovely and refreshing—like something I'd seen on a postcard back in the States. A busy terminal hummed with locals and tourists alike, and The Kowloon Star Ferry docked before a crowd of passengers stepped off.

I walked past the terminal and found myself on an upscale street, glancing into the fancy restaurant windows on either side of me. Well-dressed businessmen sat at round tables for working lunches and couples shared noodle plates in padded corner booths. Whiffs of shrimp dumplings and savory vegetables tempted me inside, but I continued walking.

For a moment, thoughts of Scarlett subsided. I strolled freely with a quiet mind, no agenda or persistent fears to dictate me. But as I went back to my hotel hours later, the thoughts returned. My tentative plan hung steadily above my head as I tried anxiously to avoid it. The more I tried to ignore it, the more I felt its heaviness. In this new place, with its bright lights and unmistakable boldness, there was absolutely no turning back now.

Chapter 32

SCARLETT

Rustic brick overlays, solid oak doors, and cornflower blue awnings. The film set is a perfect combination of authentic and picturesque. Our art director definitely outdid himself this time. I smile at a group of actors running lines. Sometimes, the set feels more like home than anywhere else.

I stroll down the sheltered street and head to costuming. *What extravagant dress have they designed for me this time?* I love the feeling of the exotic fabrics and elaborate embellishments against my skin.

Before I open the door, a pudgy hand grabs my arm. "There you are," my agent barks.

I roll my eyes. "What is it, Joe?"

"Explain this to me," he says, slamming a British gossip magazine cover against the wall.

Scarlett Daniels Leaves Producer James Carlyle

I roll my eyes again, making sure Joe sees me do it this time. "This is rubbish."

"I know it is. I just called James myself."

"Then what's the problem?"

"Don't make me say it." His voice softens.

Joe had recently become one of the few people privy to my secret.

"I just—"

"I know it's hard. I do. But this is different now, Scarlett. You're *married*."

I give him nothing but a blank stare.

"W—well," he stutters. "You know what I mean."

"I know." I nod.

"As far as the public is concerned, James isn't just a fling you can leave behind after a drunken night in Cabo—"

"*Christ*, Joe. I know that."

We both know that none of my flings have been with men.

"Sweetheart," he says, placing a hand on my tensed shoulder.

Joe has been a faithful agent for years. I honestly don't understand how he still gets me into big pictures. *Me*, with my wrinkled skin and graying hair—dyed blonde of course. He's a miracle worker. Joe has his bad-tempered moments, but I know he's always coming from a good place. The thing is, he doesn't truly understand how it feels to continually repress this. He *can't* understand.

"What do you want me to do here?"

"It's just a magazine." I shrug.

"You and I both know that's not true."

I break eye contact and stare at the cobblestone ground.

"Talk to James. He needs to know what he really signed up for."

Deep down, I know he's right. But I also know how James will react. As I walk back to our hotel, I mentally draft a press release about our broken marriage.

Chapter 33

LIA

I passed a few solitary days getting to know more of Hong Kong. I had convinced myself that I might as well explore the area and become familiar with it. It was a decent way to waste time until I figured out what to do about Scarlett. Step after step, I meandered through different neighborhoods and obscure parts of the colony.

Without a map or guide, I strolled down alleyways, through tunnels, and across squares. Old women clicked Mahjong tiles from open cottage windows. They shot me curious looks, but eventually returned their attention to the table in front of them. Children played games on sidewalk corners and ate steamed buns from local food stalls. They stared as I walked by, whispering secrets to each other as I went. I smiled as a little girl—no more than six years old—ran up to me and held out her hand expectantly.

She had disheveled black hair and wore a torn dress. I fumbled through my purse, realizing that I hadn't yet exchanged currency at the hotel. Hesitant to give her American money, I pulled out an unopened pack of M&Ms. My eternal sweet tooth planned to eat them on my last flight, but never actually got around to it. I wished that I had something else to give, but her eyes lit up when she saw the American candy. I placed the package in her tiny hands and smiled. She looked up at me with sweet dark eyes. As I went to close my purse, I saw an unwritten postcard from the first airplane. I pulled it out and gave it to her, pointing up at the sky when she furrowed her brow. She squeezed my pinky finger gently and smiled before running back to her friends.

I continued walking towards a cluster of short buildings. Bright banners with Chinese characters hung from rooftops in the thick air. Sweat tickled the nape of my neck as I peered into open shop windows. Stacks of herbs and medicines lined the walls of one store, while Chinese newspapers and books filled another. Canary-yellow window frames caught my eye as I gazed into a little bakery on the corner. There were glazed pastries covered in sesame seeds, sticky golden gelatins, and sugary buns dripping with sweet bean paste. I licked my lips and savored the thought of sinking my teeth into a fresh egg tart. But I kept walking, headed towards a tall monument in a busy square ahead.

I encountered an upscale area next, with nicely dressed men sitting on restaurant patios, drinking Chinese beer and reading the paper. Some of them seemed misplaced, while others looked oddly comfortable in the stifling heat. I felt like the mile I'd just walked had taken me to a completely different place. It's interesting how big cities tend to do that—they combine mismatched slivers of rich and poor, happy and sad.

I planned to stop for a drink until I found myself nearing

what appeared to be the end of the road. I had no idea where I was, and the distance held nothing more than fields and dust. I squinted as the midday sun hit my eyes, but could barely make out farmhouses in the rural expanse.

I turned around to retrace my steps and noticed a tiny restaurant on the next corner. A sign hanging above the red awning said "MAC's," with a few Chinese characters underneath. My achy feet needed a rest, so I walked inside and waited at the chipping countertop.

"G'day, love," said a husky Australian voice.

I whipped around to see a stocky old man standing behind me. He was carrying a crate of brown eggs.

"Oh, hello," I said, caught off guard.

"Don't let the accent fool ya," he grinned. "I make a mean hot pot . . . or whatever else you might want."

"Sounds good," I smiled and sat down at a small table near the back.

"Mac's sampler platter coming right up." He winked before disappearing into the kitchen.

I draped my fuchsia wrap over the chair and set my bark cloth purse on the seat next to me. The weather in Hong Kong waxed and waned much like it did in New York, going from cool and breezy to sweltering hot in less than an hour.

In less than fifteen minutes, Mac emerged from the kitchen with an oversized tray balanced on his right arm. He was wearing a white cloth jacket and a makeshift chef's hat. I scanned the contents as he slowly lowered his tray.

"Here ya go, love," he said proudly before identifying each dish. "Chinese pan-fried noodles," he said, his plump finger hovered over a steamy plate. "Wok-seared vegetables." He motioned to a bowl of vivid carrots, mushrooms, and squash. "Sweet and sour pork—with a Mac twist of course."

My mouth was beyond watering now.

"And fresh egg tarts." He gestured to a plate of bright yellow pastries. "The soldiers loved 'em—they couldn't get enough."

"Everything looks incredible," I said eagerly. "Thank you."

"Enjoy!"

Mac sang as he made his way back to the kitchen.

I swooped up a clump of sizzling noodles and gulped them down, relishing their saltiness and texture before moving onto the pork. My teeth chewed quickly as new flavors danced around my mouth. I couldn't get enough. I had almost devoured the entire vegetable bowl before Mac's voice pulled me out of my haze.

"Like it, do ya?" He stood next to me, trying not to laugh at my overeagerness.

"Mmm. Yes." I nodded, and my cheeks flushed hot red.

"Mind if I sit?"

"No, not at all."

Mac took the chair across from me and picked up an egg tart. "I don't even know your name," he said jovially.

"Michelle," I said quickly. I didn't know why I lied.

"Where ya from, Michelle?" he asked as he stuffed the pastry into his mouth. He was a bit rough and ragged, but there was something about him I really liked.

"New York City," I said as I wiped my mouth. "And you?"

"Sydney, originally. Moved to England as a lad. Then started with the Navy once I was old enough."

"The Navy sounds exciting."

"It is at first. But it's a dangerous life once your priorities change. My daughter was born at sea."

"Oh wow, really?"

"Yep," he said with a twinkle in his eye. "She's all grown up now, though."

"Is that how you discovered Hong Kong? The navy, I mean."

"Yep. Fell in love with this place. The people, the climate, the food . . ." He pointed to his belly and we both smiled.

"It's a captivating city," I agreed.

"I worked as a cook on the ship, so I figured I'd open up a restaurant here. Almost got kicked out when the occupation started in '41, but convinced 'em to let me stay. And the rest is history!"

I nodded and looked around at the empty tables. Everything he said almost seemed too simple. Despite Mac's amazing food, I wondered how much business he really got.

"So. How about you?"

"Me?"

"What's a nice American girl doing all the way on the other side of the world?"

I looked down and smiled when he said the word *girl*.

"Well." I struggled to think of a believable reason. "I—"

Just then, the bells on Mac's front door jingled and someone walked in. I sat up straighter in my seat and turned toward the blinding sunlight. All I could see was a silhouette.

"Hey, you!" Mac called.

I still couldn't see anything but sunlight streaming in through the large windows.

"Hey there," said a casual British voice.

Mac jumped up and met the woman by the counter. He embraced her and led her over to my table.

"Hun," he said, his arm around her shoulder, "I'd like you to meet—"

"Lia," Scarlett said, her face white.

For the first time in our lives, we were both equally stunned.

"Scarlett," I said, a gasp escaping me.

"Lia?" Mac cut in. "I thought your name was Michelle."

I opened my mouth and waited for words to come. They didn't.

"Dad? We need a minute," Scarlett whispered.

"You two know each other?" Mac asked.

Apparently he was as confused as I was. Scarlett nodded without taking her eyes off me. Mac retreated to the kitchen, muttering to himself as he went.

"What on *earth* are you doing here?" Scarlett asked. I couldn't read her tone.

"I, um—"

"Please tell me that this is a coincidence," she said hopefully.

But Scarlett knew exactly what I wasn't saying. She knew I'd followed her across the world.

"*Jesus*, Lia. How did you even know where I was?"

I broke our mutual gaze and looked down at the white linen napkin on my lap. It was stained with something dark, maybe plum sauce.

"Please tell me, Lia. How did you find out?"

"Robbie . . ."

"*Robbie?* That guy you used to date?"

"His friend sort of . . . his friend has a source." I felt her green eyes burning into me but continued to avoid them. "He told me where you were filming, and—"

"And you've been wandering the streets aimlessly, trying to hunt me down ever since?"

Scarlett let a furtive smile creep across her lips.

"I—I saw you walking the other day. At the market."

"Of course you did." She sighed.

"How can you just strut around in public? Aren't you afraid that someone might notice you?"

"First of all," she said straight-faced, "I don't *strut*. And second, it's my *job* to get noticed."

We both started laughing. It was a small chuckle at first, but then it became a full-blown, gut-wrenching kind of laugh. The kind that makes your eyes water and your stomach ache. For a moment, I felt like we were back at Oxford, in those early days of our friendship. Before it all became so serious.

WE sat at that tiny table for two hours. Mac eventually brought us oolong tea and fortune cookies. I was so lost in our conversation that I'd forgotten all about him.

"If there's anything else ya need . . ." He lingered, his curiosity getting the best of him.

"Dad." Scarlett put her manicured hand on his arm. "This is Lia."

"Well, we were talking before you arrived and—"

"*Lia*, Dad."

I watched his face change as she said my name—first filled with confusion, then bright with recognition.

"You're . . ."

I looked at Scarlett, then back at Mac.

"It's okay," she said. "He knows."

"You're *the* Lia?"

Mac's green eyes twinkled with subtle tears as I nodded. "My god," he said. He stepped closer and put his weathered hand on my shoulder. Scarlett smiled at him as she blinked back tears. Slow understanding coursed through me as I realized that Scarlett had never really forgotten about me after all. The moment was almost too much.

Later that evening, she told me all about Mac and growing up on the sea. Her face glowed as she talked about the rough waters and almost falling overboard on her seventh birthday.

"Why didn't you ever tell me?" I asked.

"Shame," she answered.

"But—"

"Until about fifteen years ago, I didn't even know my father was alive."

"What do you mean?"

"My mother died when I was ten," Scarlett said sadly. "My father wanted to keep me, but it was too hard with his new crew. He sent me to live with my aunt in England to be 'properly raised.'"

"I'm sorry," I said gently.

She looked at me and slid her fingers underneath my hand. Her forgotten touch was electric.

"I planned to go back to him the second I turned sixteen . . ."

"What happened?"

Our fingers were intertwined now.

"She told me . . . she told me that he died at sea. I didn't believe her, but two men came to our door and—"

She took back her hand to wipe her eyes.

"His ship went under, but somehow he survived."

"Didn't he ever write to you?"

"Yes, but my aunt burned his letters." There was a bitterness in her voice now. "Sad what happens, isn't it? When people interfere . . ."

"Yes." I sighed, trying to let the sadness roll off me.

"Anyway," she said, "we found each other again and here we are. That's all that matters now."

"Yes," I whispered as I reached for her other hand.

It was only when she pulled away that it dawned on me that Scarlett wasn't talking about *us*.

"We should get together again before you leave," she said, smiling. I couldn't tell if she was being genuine or just cordial.

"I'd like that," I said.

Scarlett nodded and took a long sip of tea.

"What does your fortune say?" I asked.

She cracked open a cream-colored cookie and read it aloud: "Great love will test you before it returns for good."

She laughed and tossed the tiny white paper onto the table.

"Fortunes aren't even a tradition here, you know. But my father loves them," she said, shrugging her slender shoulders.

I just stared at her, wanting desperately to live within the warmth of her green eyes and hoping that just maybe, fortunes could come true.

Chapter 34

SCARLETT

Our inevitable fight is over, and I'm leaving the hotel. I told James I'd find a different place to stay. He was so angry, so bitter, and I didn't want to risk running into him if I didn't have to.

I'll stay with my father. It makes the most sense. I'm walking straight to his restaurant, a perfectly isolated place to sleep. I didn't even bother to pack up my things—Joe will probably send a poor assistant to collect them. Usually I would take a taxi, but I like walking around here. The hot air distracts me from everything going on inside my head.

I saw my dad just last week for dinner. James doesn't know about him, of course. No one really does. He's a treasure of a man, my father. I don't want to subject him to the confusing secrets of my overcomplicated life. He missed so much of my childhood, and part of me still wants to be his little girl.

He *does* know that I'm gay, though. It's the one thing that's really strengthened our relationship, his unconditional acceptance of me. I even told him about Lia. *God*, that was a tough conversation.

I finally make it to the restaurant, drained and sweaty from the heat. The door feels heavier than usual when my tired hand pulls it open. I squint as my eyes adjust to the dim indoor light. There's a woman talking to my dad. I walk toward them and don't believe it. It's Lia. *My* Lia.

Chapter 35

LIA

We made plans to meet at Mac's restaurant the following week. In the meantime, I kept exploring a new area each day. I was really starting to like Hong Kong. In a strange way, it reminded me of Scarlett: it was mysterious, charming, and unpredictable.

No sooner had I walked into Mac's than the owner himself greeted me.

"Hey there, *Michelle.*"

I looked at him sideways and opened my mouth.

"Only kidding!" he said with a grin.

"Oh." I relaxed. "You got me!"

We both laughed before sitting down at a two-seater.

"Meeting Scarlett here, are ya?"

"Yes." I smiled. "At four o'clock."

"She'll likely be running late." He shook his head. "They work my girl too damn hard. Always another scene to film."

I looked down at my watch and hoped that he was wrong. My last meeting with Mac had been awkward, to say the least, and I had no idea how much Scarlett had revealed to him about our past.

"You okay?"

I nodded. I must have looked as uncomfortable as I felt.

"So, Lia." He held my gaze. "I don't want to pry. But I love my daughter very much. She told me about what happened all those years ago, and—"

A clattering in the kitchen startled us both.

"One of the clumsy busboys," he said casually. "Anyway. I don't understand how—"

"The letter?" I chimed in.

He nodded.

"I guess Scarlett didn't tell you that she and I met up in London. But that was almost twenty years ago . . ."

Mac shook his head, looking entirely befuddled.

"I never received her letter."

He looked even more confused now, furrowed brow and all. I wondered why Scarlett didn't tell him the whole story.

"My parents . . ." I sighed, surprised at how hard it still was to talk about. "They intercepted it because—"

The confusion vanished, and Mac nodded with understanding. "I'm sorry," he said, placing his wrinkled hand over mine.

"I loved your daughter very much. I still do."

He squeezed my hand twice before releasing it to rub his scruffy face.

I wasn't sure what had changed, but my nervousness was gone. Maybe it was Mac's kind smile, but all I could do was tell him the truth.

Scarlett arrived hours late that evening, just as her father had predicted. "Sorry," she called as she rushed in.

I turned to take in the sight of her. Faded makeup with blond waves dancing over a pair of tanned shoulders. A cherry sundress highlighted her tiny waist before falling delicately around her hips. Behind her, the bright sun was setting, revealing a radiant night sky. It was the first time I'd really noticed the stars since arriving in Hong Kong. They were even brighter than London's—light, luminous, and gleaming.

I felt the familiar sensation of my heart beating too quickly.

"You're still here," she said, beaming. "I thought for sure you would have left by now!"

"We had a date," I said, smiling.

"We did," she agreed. She set her wicker bag on an empty chair and pulled off a pair of gold clip-on earrings. "Hope you weren't bored out of your mind waiting," she said as she dropped the jewelry into her purse.

"Actually, I had a nice conversation with your father."

A blend of surprise and disbelief marred her serene expression.

"Don't worry," I said. "He told me all of your embarrassing childhood secrets."

She laughed hesitantly. "So what *did* you two talk about?"

"Us," I said honestly.

She nodded and sat down across from me. "My father is oddly accepting."

"I like him."

Scarlett tapped her red nails on the white linen tablecloth.

I couldn't help but notice that her wedding ring was missing. She was wearing it the week before, when we first met at Mac's.

As if sensing my revelation, she shrugged. "We ended it."

"I—I'm sorry," I said quietly. Divorce was a big deal.

"Are you?" she challenged.

I stared at her left hand and shook my head.

We sat in silence until a group of British soldiers stumbled by, drunk and singing war songs. They peered into the restaurant as they passed, and I stiffened in my seat. I didn't relax until the sound of their voices faded from hearing.

"So," I said. "What happened with you and James?"

"Oh, the usual."

I didn't know what she meant.

"It got too hard to *pretend*," she said flatly.

"Do you two have any children?"

"God no!" She let out a strident laugh.

I felt relief rush through my core.

"But you *were* married?"

Scarlett stared off into space. Minutes passed before she spoke again.

"It wasn't real," she whispered. "None of it."

I didn't understand. "Scarlett—"

"Oh, Lia. I can't act like I don't still have feelings for you . . ."

Those words exhilarated me. I looked up and met her emerald eyes. "Then don't."

⚹

We fell into a comfortable routine after that. I stayed with Scarlett in the spare room upstairs and Mac slept in his apartment next door. In the mornings, we would sip jasmine tea and talk about our years apart. There was so much we didn't know about each other.

Then Scarlett would leave for filming and I would help Mac in the restaurant. I was wrong about business being slow. On the contrary, the place was pretty crowded from morning until early evening. People came in every day, each one ordering dozens of egg tarts and shrimp dumplings. I got to know a few of the regulars and really started to feel at home, as strange as that sounds.

We all ate together when Scarlett returned home, usually around sundown. Mac tried to stay out of the way as much as possible, bless his heart. He probably thought that she and I were picking up where we left off. But the truth was, our shared room had an invisible line drawn down the middle. Scarlett liked her space, and I didn't want to overstep.

It was nice to have her back as a friend—though after a few weeks, I started to wonder if we were just that: friends. Aside from our conversation weeks earlier, she'd never said anything about her feelings for me. I was growing impatient, despite my best attempts to give her enough time. *What are we doing? Where are we headed?*

I often found myself awake at night, afflicted with doubts. I'd look over and see Scarlett sleeping soundly across the room. All I wanted to do was crawl into her bed and lie next to her like I used to. *Maybe then I would sleep peacefully.* Instead, I turned over and wondered what dreams were dancing through Scarlett Daniels's head.

Chapter 36

It was a particularly hazy December morning. Heavy fog swaddled the restaurant as regular customers slipped in and out. After peeling onions until my own hands started to peel, I went upstairs and showered, then slipped into a maroon swing dress and black Mary Janes. I even applied an expensive lipstick my mom had gifted me the previous Christmas. As I glanced in the floor-length mirror on Scarlett's side of the room, I smiled. My style was a far cry from thirty years ago. I ran my fingers over my loose pin curls and strutted back downstairs.

Mac whistled as I passed the kitchen, sending me into a laughing fit. I told him that I was going to explore for the rest of the day. "Be careful," he said in a serious tone that caught my attention. I got the sense that he knew what I was really up to.

After my feet got tired, I hired a rickshaw to take me the rest of the way. Xiu was a slim man, but extremely strong and fast. It was an incredible way to see more of the area. I looked up instead of straight ahead as we raced through a cobblestone square. Afternoon light spilled over the tops of the hotels and apartments towering over us. The rush of thick air tickled my nose, and my eyes began to water.

Xiu quickly turned the corner and a multihued market

came into view. Bright pink flags fluttered between aqua tents as clumps of people pushed their way through craft stalls and food carts. He called back and told me it was a holiday festival. I made a mental note to go back another day. Before I could ask him more about it, we arrived at my destination: Scarlett's film set.

⁂

I watched in wonder as Scarlett became her character. The last time I'd seen her act was 1919. I'd never quite been able to bring myself to go to the theatre to see her movies after we parted. Seeing her on that set in Hong Kong was like reading my favorite book. Her ivory dress billowed in the wind as she strolled down the busy cobblestone street. She stared off into the distance, humming softly, until someone yelled, "Cut!"

At that Scarlett visibly relaxed and turned back to her co-star. He said something inaudible, and she tossed her head back in laughter. Then she reached down to adjust her silver brace-let. I recognized it and immediately thought back to her story about Lucy. I stared at her fingers, watching them trace the scripted L, as a woman wielding fluffy powder brushes applied extra makeup to Scarlett's already flawless face.

Then I looked up from her hands and our eyes locked. My heart skipped two beats as I searched her expression. Her eyes looked different than they used to. I remembered them being bright and sparkly when I fell in love with her. Now they were deeper, like the sea, but still as vivid green as ever.

She didn't return my smile, and though her face remained calm, I quickly realized that she was upset. With the slightest shake of her head, I was cast off. I stood there, lost in a mass of excited onlookers. As I turned to leave, I thought about what she'd so assuredly told me the previous month. *No one knows me in Hong Kong.* I had a feeling that was about to change.

※

HOURS later, I was back in the restaurant at a lonely table, sitting in the same clothes I had so enthusiastically picked out earlier. The dress still looked flawless, but my wind-rustled hair, smeared makeup, and puffy eyes ruined the effect of the ensemble.

Mac was still busy in the kitchen; groups of soldiers had been trailing in and out all day.

"You all right, miss?" a nice-looking man asked.

I continued to stare despondently into my teacup, examining the saturated rouge smeared along its rim.

After another failed attempt, he sighed and moved on.

"Good-bye, then."

I didn't even notice the light outside fading to dark. All I could do was replay Scarlett's actions in my head. *Why was she angry?* I stayed in that consuming zone until a familiar voice pulled me out of it.

"There you are!"

I looked up for the first time in hours. Scarlett had barely cleared the doorway, gray leather purse in tow. Her ivory dress fluttered as she marched towards me. "I've been looking *everywhere*. But of course you'd be here!"

The remaining diners quickly cleared out, probably frightened by her fuming tone.

I sat still, not saying a word.

She dumped her purse by the stairs and marched over to me. "*So.* Why did you come to the set?"

"I . . . wanted to see you."

Her face softened. "Lia . . ."

"I didn't realize that you would be so upset."

She put her hand on my shoulder and sat down next to me. "I went to see Will recently."

I looked up from my tepid tea.

"Yes," she said. "Will Masterson, from Oxford." She picked up the teapot and poured herself a cup of oolong. "I went to visit him earlier this year, before I flew to Hong Kong."

I wasn't sure why she was telling me this.

"But he wasn't there. I contacted his parents and they . . ." She set down her cup and stopped talking.

"What happened, Scarlett?" I couldn't fill in the pieces myself.

"He was . . . lobotomized." She sniffled.

"Oh god," I said, stunned. "*Why?*"

"They told me where he was, and I went to see him. He was this bright, funny, intelligent man, Lia. And now he's sitting in a padded room, lifeless."

I had so many questions. *Lobotomized?* I wanted to comfort her, but we had only just started talking again. I was afraid of scaring her off before she fully let me back in. I reached for her hand, expecting her to pull away. She didn't. So we sat there in silence, holding hands, mourning Will together.

Chapter 37

SCARLETT

We're in the middle of filming, but I'd rather be anywhere else. I can't stop thinking about her, especially now that we're both living above my father's restaurant. My lines are memorized to the point where I can deliver them while thinking about Lia.

The director yells *Cut!* and we finally take a break. My famous costar makes a poor joke, but I force myself to laugh. After all, connections are everything in this industry. You're only celebrated until you become irrelevant.

I turn my head and see her standing there, fifty yards away. She's wearing a striking maroon dress and heels. My jaw drops open as a makeup artist begins reapplying rouge and lip color. She doesn't notice me staring until after the artist moves away.

Our eyes lock and I subtly shake my head. She looks so hopeful standing there. *But what the hell is she thinking?* We can't be seen together in public, much less on set. It's just too risky. Poor Joe is still reeling from my breakup with James.

Before she leaves, her eyes fixate on my silver bracelet. I'm sure she remembers the cuff I used to wear in remembrance of Lucy. But the thing is, this is a different bracelet. I had it made shortly after I left Oxford. The *L* stands for *Lia*.

Chapter 38

LIA

It took another week for the film set incident to fully blow over, during which time there was more silence between us than usual. And then, one day, Scarlett finally started talking again.

"Lia," she whispered one morning as I woke up slowly.

"Hmm?" I rolled over and rubbed my tired eyes.

"I just didn't want anyone to see us," she said in a hushed voice.

It seemed so out of the blue. The sky was still dark and I was half asleep.

"You don't have to—"

"I do," she insisted. "It was wrong of me to ignore you."

"Scarlett." I could barely see her face. But maybe that was how she wanted it.

"Please, Lia. Let me explain."

I nodded and sat up.

"I want to see you," she continued. "I *do*."

"I know, Scarlett."

"But Clyde Martin is my director. He's . . . very strict. And if anyone ever saw us—"

"I get it," I said firmly.

"I don't know if you do," she whispered. I felt the bed shift as she sat down next to me.

"I want to be with you."

Those words were espresso for my heart. I sat up straight and looked at her in the darkness.

"I really do, Lia."

I didn't know what to say.

"I know that I've given you mixed signals." She sighed. "But I've been scared about—"

"People seeing us."

"Yes." She exhaled and moved closer.

I glanced out the tiny bedroom window next to us. The sun was starting to come up. Heavy clouds parted to expose a pale sherbet sky.

"Maybe this can be our Wonderland," she whispered.

I wasn't entirely sure what she meant. If I thought about it harder, maybe I would have understood. But I didn't want to. I wanted to accept whatever she was proposing. I craved the connection we used to have. I wanted to take yards from the inches she had given me. So I stopped thinking, and I kissed her in the smoky sunrise.

It was hesitant at first—respectful, even. Scarlett's lips received mine cautiously. But then she kissed me back, and it became a kiss so bold and passionate that I wondered if maybe we really had gone back in time. We were those two girls again, our fiery hearts beating for each other in love and lust.

The rest of the day was magic. Scarlett had time off from filming, so we took a boat ride around Middle Bay. The driver was unfazed by our giddy laughter and girlish behavior, although we probably looked quite foolish as grown women. I didn't care, though, because I hadn't felt so alive in years. We didn't even hold hands, but it reminded me of what a real date with her might feel like. I wanted more.

"So," I asked over breakfast the next morning. "What exactly is your film about?"

"It's an adventure with a bit of romance," she said dryly.

"Sounds exciting," I said, beaming. "I can't wait to see it."

She didn't even look up from her tea. "The thing is," she finally said, "I'm not very impressed with the script."

"Oh?"

"I used to take roles for their depth and grit. And now I just take parts for parts. The industry isn't exactly kind to its *aging actresses*. . ."

I glanced at her, wondering if she was exaggerating.

"I remember being at Oxford in that first play . . . the exhilaration that came with being onstage."

"I remember watching you act for the first time." I smiled.

"I remember you being there." Her eyes lit up. "I was so proud."

"You're a movie star, Scarlett," I said matter-of-factly. "You *made* it."

"Then why am I so unhappy, Lia?"

I felt my heart sink a little.

"Why am I so unfulfilled with this career? This life?"

She looked at me with inquisitive eyes. I wanted to state

the obvious, but I didn't know how. I wanted to propose that *love* was actually the answer to her unanswerable question. But instead, I stayed silent. Still, as the hushed air enveloped us, I got the feeling she knew exactly what I was thinking.

Chapter 39

As December unfolded, I couldn't help but think about home. The holidays, with the striking seasonal weather and festive winter decorations, were my favorite time of year. I loved spending time at my parents' house during this time of year, stringing bright lights around places they could no longer reach, sitting by the crackling fire, and sipping hot chocolate, just like we did when I was a little girl. Being with my parents brought a certain comfort that only family could. And I missed them dearly. My dad and I had parted on good terms, but I hadn't seen my mother since the restaurant incident. I wondered if she hated me. Regardless of what happened, I could never hate her.

I closed my eyes and thought about being back in New York. *Dad trimming the tree, Mom and I baking gooey cinnamon rolls in the kitchen as winter spices drift through the air . . .*

That was it, wasn't it? *Comfort.* The one thing Scarlet had never given me. She loved me, yes. My time with her was always spontaneous and electrifying. But she never reassured me. Maybe the chase was what had kept me going all these years. I still loved her like I loved her then. But what if love wasn't enough?

I shook my head and opened my eyes. Warm rain fell softly

against the dirty windowpane. Maybe I was just too alone with my thoughts. I considered going downstairs, but Mac was out fishing and the restaurant was closed for the day. Scarlett had told me she would be filming until sundown.

I had actually been looking forward to some time alone, but now all I could think about was my failed plan. I had been there more than a month. *Has anything even changed?* I wanted to believe that things were different, I really did. But I couldn't seem to convince myself of it.

I wished so badly that I could go into town and talk to her, but of course I couldn't go anywhere near the movie set—she'd made that crystal clear. I'd accepted it at the time, but now the thought was frustrating me beyond belief. *She wants me cooped up here.* It was Scarlett's ideal setup: she got to prance around with her fellow movie stars all day long, and then come home to me. I was sure it was all very wonderful for her. But on my end, it was hell.

Then I realized exactly where I was. I was in Wonderland. A secret little world where we could be ourselves, but only until the sun came up, and then we had to go back to pretending. She had even mentioned it when we were talking. *Maybe this can be our Wonderland.* Why had I brushed it off like an afterthought? Fear pulsed through me as I sat on my depressing twin bed. *Why is this happening again?* In the end, Wonderland burned down anyway.

I looked out the tiny bedroom window and peered up into Hong Kong's cloudy sky. It was nearly dark now, and a gray murkiness was moving slowly through the air. I sighed and pulled down the shade before drifting into a soundless slumber. I knew that no matter how long I waited, I wouldn't find the stars that night.

A thunderstorm woke me up the next day. I rolled over and pulled up the window shade, revealing a mass of intimidating dark clouds. It was probably after noon, but the obscure sky made it impossible to tell. Scarlett was already gone; a pile of couture clothes on her unmade bed clued me into a frantic morning. I smiled as I thought of her holding each piece up to her body, then frowning and tossing it aside, trying to find something that would make her look more stunning. She never realized that it was an unattainable feat. It was she who made the clothes look beautiful, not the other way around.

I finger-combed my hair and pulled it into a messy ponytail. Mac wouldn't care how I looked, and I was too tired to fully get ready. I threw on a robe before tiptoeing downstairs.

I entered the room cautiously, but my shoulders relaxed when I realized that no one was dining. The storm had probably deterred anyone from venturing out so far.

"There she is," Mac said before gulping down the rest of his black coffee. He was sitting in his favorite corner table near the kitchen, reading a tattered book.

I smiled. "Hi."

"Haven't seen you in years," he teased.

I rolled my eyes and walked over to him.

"You shoulda come fishin' with me yesterday," he said as I sat down. "Great catches out there."

"I'm sorry." I sighed. "I was tired."

He looked at me and tilted his head, ocean eyes duller than usual. "What's goin' on?"

I broke eye contact and looked into the storm. "Just . . . tired. Maybe it's the time change," I muttered.

"Nah, that's not it." He shook his head.

I shrugged and tried to change the subject. "So you had a good catch yesterday?"

He just stared at me. Mac rarely pried, but I could tell he wasn't going to let this go.

"I'm just . . . sad. I miss home, and—"

"Is it Scarlett?"

"No," I lied.

He remained painfully silent.

"Yes," I said quietly.

Mac nodded as if he'd known all along, but said, "I thought you two were getting along great."

"We are. It's not that. It's—"

A boom of thunder startled us both.

"It's . . ."

"You want *more*."

I felt like Mac was reading my mind. Surprisingly, it didn't bother me. He reminded me of my own father, and there was something endearing about him. I felt like I could trust him.

"Yes," I said.

Mac nodded again. "I understand. Scarlett isn't exactly forthcoming with her emotions. Never has been."

I looked down as the rain grew louder.

"She does have a big heart though, Lia."

"I know," I whispered.

"I'm not saying it'll be easy," he said. "But you have to tell her how you're feeling. She might not even realize how upset you are."

I looked at him and wondered if I should talk about what happened *before* she sent that letter. I wanted to tell him about our final conversation, about how Scarlett had so suddenly changed her mind. But I didn't want to slight his little girl's big heart. So I nodded instead.

The afternoon dragged on slowly as sheets of rain plastered Mac's restaurant. Continuous thunder ruined my plan of sleeping through the rest of the day. I kept thinking about Oxford and our relationship. *Is it possible that I still think we're something we can never be?*

⁂

I had no choice but to confront Scarlett when she came home the next evening. The sound of her footsteps startled me awake from my disorienting nap. I hadn't left the room all day. The door swung open and there she was, dripping wet in a pair of shiny navy oxfords.

"Hey!" she said cheerfully and set her wet umbrella on the squeaky floor. Her blond locks were matted with wind and rainwater.

"Hi," I said softly.

She walked over to me and kissed the top of my head. I wondered how her mere presence could wash away the doubts that had been festering in my mind all day.

"How was everything?" she asked as she hung her olive coat up to dry.

"It was . . . fine." I sighed. "How was filming?"

She proceeded to tell me all about it. But for the first time, I didn't hear a word she said. I sat there as Scarlett talked, observing her understated movements and smiling as she threw her head back and laughed. I watched the flicker in her eyes and the curve of her pink smile, the way she used her hands to emphasize a point. *Why have I never noticed that before?*

"I'm going to shower off," she called as she left the room.

I nodded, still lost in Scarlett's subtleties. The rain came back into earshot as I heard the familiar sound of thunder above us. Despite the doubtful cloud looming over my head, I was undeniably falling back into blinding love.

Chapter 40

Christmas arrived, and with it a break from Scarlett's hectic film schedule.

"We finish shooting next month," she said contentedly as we assembled our makeshift holiday meal.

Mac seasoned fish in garlic and basil while Scarlett and I roasted vegetables and rolled sticky dinner buns. We even baked a plum cake for dessert. It was the greatest thing I could have hoped for. In less than two months, they had become my second family.

"That's wonderful." Mac beamed. "I'm proud of you, honey."

Scarlet leaned over and kissed his cheek before winking at me. "That means I'll have much more free time, Lia."

My mind cycled through a thousand scenarios during dinner, each involving Scarlett. *We might stay a while longer in Hong Kong before returning home. Or we could trek through Southeast Asia together before exploring another part of the globe. Maybe we'll fly straight back to the States and divide our time between New York and London.* The possibilities made my heart flutter.

Scarlett and I offered to clean so Mac could go to sleep early. I hugged him good night before he grabbed his coat and went next door. Chilled wind rushed in behind him before we locked up.

I lathered dish soap in my hands as I scrubbed each pot and pan. Scarlett dried them before putting every dish into its place. Our fingers brushed together as I handed her a pair of wineglasses, sending ripples up my forearm.

After the place was spotless, we walked leisurely upstairs. I showered and changed into a satin nightshirt before returning to our shared room. Scarlett sat perched atop her wooden twin bed silhouetted against the window. I hung my damp terry-cloth towel over the door and looked at her.

The scene was like a painting, low light with an actress sitting in front of the stars. Yes, *stars*. I'd only just noticed them. I stared through the window at their perfection. The callous storm had finally given way to a brilliant night sky, clearer than crystal. I wanted to paint everything and copy that perfect scene onto paper—preserve it forever. *Scarlett and the stars.*

I thought back to our conversation almost twenty years before. *You and I both realized that the world wouldn't accept what we wanted, so we swore off stars.* Believing in stars was like believing in the possibility of us. I'd never stopped believing, had I? Maybe she had sworn us off, but I never had.

Scarlett came back into focus as my imaginary painting faded. I realized that although time could be cruel, it had been kind to our bodies. I was more toned than my younger self, while Scarlett's perfect figure had only become more defined with age. I could barely resist her as I stared from across the room. She was reading her script with an unwavering focus that made me want to take it right out of her hands. I wanted her to look at me as she used to, with those seductive eyes and demure smile.

She looked up from her lines and met my gaze. Startled, I looked away and tried desperately to find a worthy distraction. But it was too late. She set the script down and stood up, giving me the opportunity to admire every inch of her. My eyes traced each delicious curve, and I instantly wished that she would take off her sheer white robe and nightgown. Scarlett tilted her head with an unreadable expression, running her silky hands along her décolletage. She stood in place for what felt like eternity. Then, before I could say anything, she walked right over to my side of the room and stood above me.

I looked up at her familiar face—a face that I had once memorized, caressed, and kissed with abandon—and stood up slowly, relishing our physical closeness. I could hear every breath Scarlett took and smell her enchanting body. That sweet scent I used to love ignited something deep within my being. I reached out for her and she came closer. To my delight, she moved the same way she had when we were younger. Her graceful limbs entangled with mine as we began to make love.

I was more confident than I had been the last time. Instead of second-guessing everything, I touched Scarlett exactly the way I wanted to. She swayed beneath me as I kissed every part of her, head to toes and back again. It felt like we were making up for lost time. I was entirely consumed in that overwhelming moment, solely aware of the woman I loved.

Chapter 41

SCARLETT

It's Christmas night, and from the beginning of the evening I'm immediately thrown back into love and lust with Lia. It's *everything*, from the way she speaks sweetly with my father to the way she kisses me good night. I even catch myself smiling at the way she sips tea after breakfast. Of course I never stopped loving Lia, but this is entirely fresh.

Hong Kong really is the perfect place. I never would have chosen it from a world map, but this city's become my favorite. I don't dread things here like I do at home. Lia and I can actually go places together without paid photographers documenting our every move. I was paranoid that day on the set, and she's proven me wrong since then.

We can actually *be together* here, unrestricted dates and all. The lack of secrecy between us is thrilling. She still has the same free spirit, but she's also an absolutely different person. The way I love her now is *nothing* like the way I loved her then. I know what I want. I want us to stay here forever.

Still, I can't stop thinking about Will. The way his parents found out . . . how they tried to "fix" him . . . how the doctors sucked the life right out of him. He's alive, but he's not really there.

I shake my head and try to stay *here*, in the present moment. Those threatening thoughts are the worst at nighttime, anyway. I look at Lia, laughing uncontrollably at something funny my father has just said. Her infectious smile begins to dissolve my fear, destroying it slowly, taking it apart at the seams.

I hope I didn't scare her when I told her about Will. She was surprised, yes. But hearing about something is *nothing* compared to seeing it. I have no doubt that the image of Will—lobotomized Will—is permanently etched in the darkest corners of my mind. It reminds me of what can happen to people like us. People like Lia. Like me.

Chapter 42

LIA

The next morning was languid and pleasant. I woke up gradually as the sun kissed my face and Scarlett's hair tickled my neck. Her warm body pressed up against mine in our newly shared twin bed. I watched her chest rise and fall as she slept.

I was tired enough to fall back to sleep, but I kept myself awake. I wanted, *needed* to enjoy every precious moment of this time with Scarlett. Her guard was down for the first time in ages. I would soak up every second of this bliss until she woke up.

Eventually, she did. By then the daylight had fully flooded our room with orangey hues. Although we couldn't exactly hear the kitchen, smells of Mac's morning baking wafted in through the pipes. I felt my stomach grumble as the sugary scent of custard tarts overtook our surroundings.

"Hungry?" Scarlett looked at me with wide eyes and a sweet smile.

"A little," I said, grinning.

She adjusted her nightgown and cuddled up closer to me. "Happy Christmas."

I looked down at her and shook my head playfully.

"I meant Happy *Belated* Christmas," she joked.

"You're cute," I said candidly.

"I still have red wine in my system from last night," she said with a wink.

We laughed, and I stroked her golden hair.

"I can't wait to be finished," she confessed.

"With the movie?"

She nodded and sat up slowly.

"What will we do then?" I rolled onto my side.

Her emerald eyes lit up. "Let's stay here forever," she purred.

"I wish." I laughed.

"I'm serious, Lia."

I sat up so that we were face-to-face. "Scarlett . . ."

"What?" Her expression was completely sober.

"You know we can't. We have to go back and face the real world."

"What do you mean?"

"It will be tough at first, but we'll get through it together," I assured her as I reached out to caress her face.

"*Christ*, Lia. We can't go back there and *be together* . . ."

She pulled away, and I felt our previous night's affection quickly evaporate. I looked at her for a lingering moment, hoping desperately that she would say something else.

"But I thought—"

"*What?*" she scoffed. "That we could live happily ever after in New York or London?"

"Well, not exactly like a fairy tale, but—"

"You just don't get it!"

Her words detonated my composure. This scene was all too familiar.

"My God, Scarlett. It's like nothing has changed!"

"I don't understand why you think that people will suddenly change their minds and accept . . . *this*."

"*This* is you and me. We're in love," I whispered.

"That doesn't mean that we can show and tell everyone," she said bitterly.

"You don't even want to try!"

"I have other things to think about—"

"Right. Like your fucking career. I guess love takes a backseat to fame."

Her face fell. "You know that's not true, Lia." She turned around, and wild blond waves tumbled over her shoulders.

"God, I'm so stupid," I cried. "It's like we're back at Oxford and I'm still that naïve girl whose heart gets broken again and again."

"Don't say that," she countered quietly.

"It's the truth, Scarlett."

"That's not fair. I don't want *either* of us to face the torment and humiliation—"

"I know, Scarlett. You only care about what the fucking world thinks."

She opened her pink lips to protest, but I turned away before she could.

I tried so hard to gather my emotions. Maybe I could leave before it was too late. I wiped my stinging eyes and watched the tears dry from my hands. All I wanted was to look at her and feel nothing. But as I lifted my head and met those know-ing green eyes, I felt the remaining pieces of my heart shatter once more.

Chapter 43

I wasn't sad. I was *enraged*. How could it be that after all these years, I was still so naïve? I should have learned my lesson when she turned me away the first time. *And the second.* But I was so certain that something had changed, that she was a different person. And now, in just a couple of blissful months, I'd let her break me again.

I wasn't sad to leave Hong Kong. Although I'd enjoyed most of my time there, New York was home. I *was* sad to leave Mac, though. When he noticed me packing up my trunk, he got a worried look on his face. I made up some lame excuse that I'm sure he didn't believe. In the moment, I didn't feel a shed of regret. It all hit me on the flight home.

Mac was one of the only two people I cared about in Hong Kong. Aside from being sweet and funny, he was a genuinely good person. He carried my trunk downstairs and drove me to the airport himself. Until that morning, I hadn't even realized that he owned a car. My anger toward Scarlett was no match for the kindness Mac had shown me.

I was determined to do anything I could to ease my pain. Unfortunately, that took the form of drowning my sorrows in cheap wine on every flight. I drank more than I should have and paid for it during my Los Angeles layover. I spent that hour hunched over a dirty toilet in the ladies' restroom. All the kneeling made my legs go numb, and the smell of urine only rendered me sicker.

Needless to say, the flight back to New York was uncomfortable. I stumbled off the plane without a fraction of dignity in tow. I'd phoned Robbie from Chicago and told him I was coming back, and he picked me up from the airport with a hopeful look on his face, awaiting at least a speck of good news. I shook my head and climbed into the front seat.

We drove silently back to Brooklyn as the clouds multiplied overhead. Robbie opened his mouth a few times to say something, but quickly recoiled when he saw my dejected face. I wouldn't, *couldn't*, talk about what happened. Not yet, anyway.

I drifted into a nap on the way back, unable to resist the tug of sleep. Maybe it was the jetlag, but I had a feeling it was something else. I woke up to Robbie rubbing my back gently. Shreds of overcast light peeked in through the car windows and my apartment building stood straight ahead.

"Let's go up," he said. "I'll grab your luggage."

I nodded and walked sluggishly inside.

Robbie set my trunk in the bedroom while I collapsed onto my couch.

"I'll make some coffee," he called from the kitchen.

"Tea," I replied weakly.

He returned minutes later with a hot mug. I took a sip of black tea and felt the warm liquid run down my dry throat.

"Get some rest, okay?" he said. "I'll check on you in a few days."

He kissed my forehead before turning to leave. I watched

him linger at the front door for a second, fingertips tracing its wooden frame. Then he shook his head and closed it gently behind him. My heavy eyelids shut against my will as I tried to say good-bye. Although I couldn't verbalize the words, I knew for certain that Robbie Wells would always be a true friend— perhaps a better one than I deserved.

Chapter 44

Brooklyn, January 1950

I woke feeling extremely disoriented. *Where am I?* I'd gotten so used to living at Mac's that I didn't even recognize my own apartment. As the past few days' events gradually became lucid, I realized that I was no longer in Hong Kong. I was no longer with Scarlett.

That fleeting awareness had little effect on my fatigued mind. I wasn't even conscious enough to fully grasp the big picture. I buried my cloudy head under a puffed throw pillow and snuggled back into the woven quilt wrapped loosely around me.

DAYLIGHT woke me up the next morning. *Or is it the ringing?* I was jolted out of an unknown dream as I heard the first high-pitched sound. My initial instinct was to feel around the coffee table. I reached my arm out abruptly, drowsy eyes still closed, but all I succeeded in doing was knock over a mug of cold tea. I cursed as the chilly liquid spilled over my icy fingertips.

Another shrill ring. I opened my eyes as widely as I could,

squinting into the bright light pouring in from the windows. A dull achiness plagued my lower back when I tried to sit up. As another ring burst through my ears, I rolled off the sofa and onto my parquet floor. The phone stopped ringing.

I put my hands to my head and rubbed my sore temples, wondering how long I'd been asleep. Thoughts of Robbie came to mind as I stared at the spilled black tea on my coffee table. After everything that happened, he still cared about me. He was there for the ups and the downs, plus everything in between. I smiled slightly at the realization.

As I continued to wake up, remnants of rage and resentment cluttered my thoughts. It was like everything *Scarlett* came rushing back at once. Fragments of our heartrending aftermath came together into something I'd denied from the beginning: the truth. No matter how much I treasured Scarlett, I couldn't change her mind.

Two quick knocks on the door brought me back to my messy apartment. I stood up and ran my fingers through my stringy, unwashed hair, reluctant to see who was there.

"Lia? You there?"

Robbie. I relaxed instantly. I swiftly turned the knob and opened my front door. Robbie was leaning against the wall outside, looking comfortable in a maroon peacoat and slacks. His tan skin was slightly worn from the war, but he could still pass for a man of forty. He looked great, despite the concerned expression lingering on his familiar face.

"Hey," he said, stepping toward me.

I threw my arms around my dear friend and he embraced me back.

"Come in," I said quietly. I took the bag of groceries he was carrying and set it on my kitchen counter. He stopped in his tracks and looked around the apartment, running a weathered hand through his dark hair.

"Lia . . . have you been out of the house since I dropped you off?"

"No," I muttered. "It's only been a couple of days—"

"It's been two weeks."

I looked at him in shock. I had no memory of waking up more than twice in all that time, a few times at most.

Without speaking, he folded up my quilt and dried up the tea on my coffee table.

"Have you even eaten?" He gestured to my shrunken frame.

I shook my head and felt my stomach grumble. "I'm a mess, Robbie," I sobbed.

He walked over and put his arm around me. "Ready to talk about it?"

I sighed and collapsed into his welcoming hug. "Okay."

I spoke until I was out of breath, rattling off every trivial detail as I took him through the previous two months. He listened patiently and nodded every now and then. After two and a half hours, I'd imparted everything I could remember.

"Please say something," I begged, desperate for some sliver of hope.

Robbie looked at me with a sad but knowing smile. "I'm sorry, Lia. But you did everything you could."

My head went numb. Somehow, hearing another person say those words was a hundred times worse than my own recognition. If even *Robbie* thought it was over, I had zero chances left.

Chapter 45

London, February 1950
SCARLETT

"Thank you, Robbie," I say before hanging up the receiver. I take a deep breath and try to steady myself. *I made the call.* There's no turning back now. Two quick honks remind me that the car is waiting downstairs. I have a flight to catch.

Chapter 46

LIA

The January weather rendered me a quiet homebody. I stayed inside and had no problem dozing past noon. This quickly turned into a lazy winter routine. I'd wake up late, sip coffee, and read all day long. It was too comfortable to change.

After missing several calls—presumably from my frantic secretary—I finally answered.

"Hello?"

"Lia? Hi! Did you extend your leave?"

Per usual, Giselle was talking a mile a minute.

"Hi. No—I'm back. Sorry for not calling."

"Oh good! I was so worried."

"Is everything okay at the office?"

"Oh yes, everything is fine. We're awfully busy without you though."

I told her that I was ill and needed some more time off. A female deputy managing editor was filling in for me, and I assured Giselle that Brianna would continue to do a great job. I had been gone longer than I would have liked, but I trusted her judgment and work ethic. After Giselle relaxed a little, I said that I would phone when I was ready to come back. It was a lie, unless you count a sick heart among excusable ailments. Missing work was completely unlike me, but I needed time to heal and reset.

Against my wishes, Robbie told my parents that I was back in town. He thought it would be good for me to be around family, even though my mother and I hadn't spoken since before I left for Hong Kong. I wasn't sure how I felt about seeing her—but I was excited to see my dad, who phoned and eagerly asked if he could bring over some lunch the day after Robbie told them I was home. I opened my door that afternoon to see him holding a fresh box of pasta. I couldn't help but smile.

"Hi, Dad."

"Lia!" He set the food down and cloaked me in a giant bear hug. When he released me, he raised his eyebrows. "So, tell me about—"

"I'd rather not talk about it, Dad. I'm just trying to . . . move on." Avoiding his gaze, I walked over to my white-washed cupboard and grabbed two plates. "I'm sorry, it's just that—"

"I understand, hun. No need to explain."

I appreciated his accepting reaction, while also realizing that Robbie had probably already filled him in on most of the story. They were always talking behind my back. I didn't mind this time, though—it was anything but malicious, and it saved me a lot of explanation I wasn't ready for.

"Fresh pasta for my Lia," my dad said as I returned with

plates and utensils, revealing our steamy lunch. Notes of thyme mingled with spiced onions in creamy mushroom sauce. My shoulders relaxed a little as I inhaled the familiar aroma.

"Mom?" I asked, already knowing the answer.

"Yep," he said quietly.

"I wish—"

"She'll come around, my love. She just needs time."

I looked down, not really believing his response.

"So," he continued. "Robbie seems happy to be hanging around again."

I nodded and swallowed my first bite of Italian noodles in months.

"He's so taken by you." My dad laughed.

"*Dad.*"

"I know, honey, it's just sweet. That boy would do anything for you."

"We're good friends," I said quickly.

"Believe me, Lia. He's more than captivated by you. Always has been."

I swallowed hard and took another bite.

"Have you ever thought about—"

"No, Dad," I said defensively. "End of discussion."

"Just a thought." He shook his head and smiled.

I knew exactly what my father was thinking. I could marry Robbie for reasons beyond love. Lots of women married for security those days, regardless of romance. But I could *never* do that to him. And more importantly, I could never do that to myself.

※

BY February, I still hadn't returned to work, but I did manage to resist the temptation to stay cooped up inside. I made plans to meet Robbie for lunch one foggy weekend afternoon. He phoned beforehand and said he'd be stopping by first. I peered out my misty window and saw his black car pull up, rubber tires crunching over the freshly laid gravel. He hopped out of the driver's seat and looked up at me. He wore a long navy winter coat and slate-gray loafers. I waved as the wind rustled his dark hair and he walked toward the front gates.

"I thought we could go into the city instead," he said, grinning, when he got upstairs. "There's a parade!"

"No way!"

"C'mon," he pleaded. "It's my turn to choose."

I stared at him for the longest time as opposing thoughts warred in my head. But finally, I conceded. "Okay," I said. "I'll grab my coat."

※

WE sped over the bridge toward New York City. Robbie turned on the car radio and we hummed along to Bing Crosby's "Only Forever." I struggled to sing in key, laughing between each chorus, but Robbie had a perfect voice, honed from years of singing in the school choir. My dad's words floated through my head every time I looked at my old friend. I turned the music up and tried to drown them out.

As the song ended, we arrived in Manhattan. I hadn't been there in months and was happy to be back. There we were, right in the midst of flashy Times Square. Jazz musicians played for tips as hot nuts roasted on street corners. Their spicy-sweet scent flooded my senses as posh couples poured in and out of Macy's. I looked around the crowded streets and then up at the buildings towering over us.

"Where's the parade, Robbie?"

"It'll be here," he said, smiling.

I watched my breath turn to clouds as chilly urban air blew by. "It's freezing," I whispered, immediately regretting not having brought gloves.

When my icy fingers went numb, Robbie told me to stay put and went to get us some coffee. I breathed into my frozen hands and noticed a little girl in a red dress. Her pigtails flopped around as she played with a shiny blue balloon. I watched in awe as she ran in circles, seemingly without a care in the world. I wished I could feel even a fraction of her whimsy. She jumped up and down between playful giggles as she pointed across the way.

"Mommy!" She tugged on a woman's maroon jacket.

The girl's mother lit up as soon as she saw what her daughter was pointing to. I wheeled around to witness the spectacle for myself.

A mass of colorful winter coats was gathering around a small stage. I couldn't make out any faces as I squinted across the square. Robbie handed me a cup of hot coffee and put his hand on my shoulder.

"Bottoms up," he said, winking.

"Thanks," I said distractedly, craning my neck to catch a glimpse of the mysterious stage.

More people stared at the stage as hushed voices multiplied across Times Square. I clutched my coffee harder and felt each finger come back to life.

"It's her!" the little girl yelled.

Robbie glanced nervously in my direction as my jaw dropped. It was *her*. It was Scarlett.

"Lia, I . . ."

Robbie's words faded into the background as I watched her take center stage. Scarlett's blond hair was pulled back into a sleek chignon, with wispy pieces peeking out from underneath her cobalt blue headscarf. She walked effortlessly up the stairs in a pair of stick thin stilettos as her rosy dress billowed in the wind.

Cameras flashed as news correspondents crowded around the stage. She seemed unfazed, the epitome of a seasoned movie star. I wanted to move closer, but my feet were firmly planted in place. I was standing close enough to see her, but far enough away so that I couldn't get hurt again.

A stocky man who I assumed to be her agent scurried up onto the stage behind Scarlett. He whispered something in her left ear; she shooed him away and stepped forward to a wooden podium equipped with microphones, causing a surge of commotion and waving hands.

"Scarlett!" shouted one newsman. "Are you really getting divorced?"

Scarlett opened her mouth as Robbie squeezed my hand.

"*Lia.* We can leave—"

I turned back to the press conference before he could say anything else. Reporters yelled over each other until a distinct question finally emerged from the chaotic mass of voices.

"Is there anyone new in your life?"

Scarlett looked down for a moment. I wondered if she was fiddling with her bracelet behind that wooden podium. Then she spoke.

"There is," she said confidently.

Reporters buzzed as gloved hands shot into the frosty city air.

"I'm in love," she continued.

My coffee dropped to the snowy ground. Hot liquid pooled around my penny loafers.

"With a woman."

Stillness inundated the crowd. For a moment, the entire square was silent.

"But the love of my life is someone I've known since I was a girl," Scarlett said steadily.

Onlookers murmured to each other as she took off her cat-eye sunglasses.

"And she needs to know . . . how sorry I am."

Caught in a moment of pure and public vulnerability, Scarlett put her sunglasses back on and walked gracefully down the stairs. Reporters swarmed as she descended the stage. I watched in awe as her agent hurried her into a black town car.

Robbie whispered something to me as spectators resumed their Saturday shopping. But all I heard was the bitter sound of the black car speeding away. I watched it drive off into the blurred distance, disappearing into a haze of rainclouds and February fog.

Chapter 47

SCARLETT

I walk quickly up the steps, one stiletto after the next. *This is it.* I'm on stage in front of Christ knows how many people. Everyone thinks actors are good public speakers, but it's quite the opposite. Playing a part is much easier than being yourself.

Joe tries to change my mind one last time. I hurry him off the platform without a second thought. The crowd swells as I look around for *her*. I only hope Robbie made good on his promise. Otherwise, this is all for nothing.

I breathe into the microphone and tell the world who I really am. It's something I should have done years ago, while I was still young. As I climb back into Joe's car, I have an unshakable feeling that I'm too late.

Chapter 48

LIA

The rest of the world came back into focus after she left. Robbie swallowed the remainder of his creamy coffee without taking his eyes off me.

"Are you okay?" he asked quietly.

I didn't respond. My mind was frozen. I wasn't really sure what had just hit me. As Robbie stared at me, waiting for a response, I looked around cautiously. A lot of people looked fine, as if nothing had happened. But others were gossiping frantically about Scarlett, enraged by the scandalous news she'd dropped five minutes prior.

I felt the color drain from my cheeks, and my face lost all feeling. I wasn't sure if the numbness was from the cold, or was the result of something else. Finally, I decided it was most likely from the realization that after thirty years, Scarlett Daniels had finally revealed the truth about us. Publicly.

"Lia!" Robbie sounded equally frustrated and concerned. *"Are you all right?"*

"No," I managed to say. "No, I'm not."

He parted his lips before quickly turning away.

"What is it?"

He didn't respond.

"Robbie?"

"She called my apartment. Told me to bring you here . . ."

My mouth went dry as the cold air chapped my lips.

"Look, I refused at first. But then she kept calling and calling. She sounded so sad and genuine, Lia. I agreed to bring you, but *Jesus*. Scarlett didn't say anything about a full-blown press conference. Sounded more like a lunch—"

"My god," I cried.

Robbie stepped closer and I moved away.

"I can't believe this!"

"Lia—"

"You too, Robbie? After you saw me broken for weeks?"

"I'm not the bad guy here," he said firmly.

"Just when I'm finally starting to heal, she creeps right back into my life!"

People started to stare as I continued to shout, but Robbie didn't seem to care about the observers. He took my hand and squeezed it tightly.

"I'm sorry. But you wanted Scarlett back in your life too. You went all the way to Hong Kong to find her."

"Before she hurt me again."

Rain prickled my forehead, and slick umbrellas began to pop up around Times Square. I wiped my eyes and heard the jazz musicians resume their tunes. Robbie put his arm around me and we walked back to the parking garage. I lingered in front of a stand with cinnamon almonds, but shook my head when he asked me if I wanted some. He started the car quickly and we left the chaos of Manhattan. As we drove across the bridge, I realized that it was Valentine's Day.

⁂

THE truth is, I didn't know how I felt. What started as shock morphed into rage and then confusion. Fear and fury and revelation raced through my mind as intrigue and doubt collided. I felt *everything*.

Robbie was right. He wasn't the bad guy here. This was a matter of good intentions and secret agendas. I knew that he had my best interests at heart. It took a few hours for me to come around, but a simple phone call was apology enough for my understanding friend.

My instinct was to drown my sorrows in a bottle of red. The couch looked so inviting, and I still had some leftover wine. But I resisted, because I knew that it was time to stop feeling sorry for myself. I'd lain around long enough. Maybe resuming my old routine would help me sort things out.

I went back to work the next morning. Giselle perked up as I walked into the office, her cherry-painted lips turning up into a grin. Articles and scribbled memos covered my mahogany desk and stained coffee cups lined the windowsill. After tidying up, I was ready to tackle my job again.

It felt great to be back. Hours passed without me even realizing it. One of the staff writers brought in tea sandwiches, so I took a break to join everyone in the lunchroom. I told my co-workers that I'd returned from an extended holiday. Most of them smiled for the sake of formality, nodding politely but not really caring about the reason.

Soon, I was back in the swing of my old schedule. I woke up early, sipped tea or coffee, and walked to the office. The cold was equally vexing and refreshing. I kept telling myself that a beautiful spring season was just around the corner. After a week or so, it felt like nothing had ever changed. I was amazed at how easy it was to fling myself into work again.

⁜

I arrived ten minutes late one morning, delayed by yet another rainstorm. Voices chirped as I approached the front door. I cracked a smile and wondered what the office was gossiping about this time. But everyone muted immediately when I walked in. I waved and took off my yellow raincoat, shaking my head slightly at their sudden silence.

I shut my office door as people continued to stare. Unfortunately, the clear glass did nothing to put me at ease. It seemed like every time I looked up, someone was gawking in my direction. Right as I was about to confront them, Giselle raced into my office. Her garnet heels made a clicking sound every time she took a step, like fingernails tapping on plastic.

"So," she said quietly. "Is it true?"

I glanced up from my reading to see her towering over my cluttered desk.

"Is what true?"

Giselle raised a pencil-thin eyebrow in disbelief. "You know . . ."

"I don't," I said as I made a quick edit on the story I was reading.

"About you and Scarlett Daniels, the *movie star*."

My pen made another pass across the page before I processed her words. "What exactly are you talking about?"

"*This*," Giselle said, planting the cover of *New York Weekly* smack in front of me. The headline read, "Famous Actress Is Homosexual."

Pictures of Scarlett took up the entire page—an old headshot from her modeling days, a snap from her latest movie set, and a recent photo taken in Times Square. I ran my fingers over the black-and-white photos, then moved my palm to reveal another image. It was a bit blurred, but I could make out two distinct faces. It was a shot of Scarlett and me in Hong Kong. A caption below read, *Daniels with her lover.* I was utterly lost for words.

"It's you! I knew it!"

Giselle clicked her heels out of my office and said something inaudible to everyone out front. I stuffed the paper into my handbag and took a deep breath. This was it, the moment I'd desired for years. The truth was finally out . . . and circulated to thousands of readers.

Gossipy voices hushed again as I stepped out of my office. I wanted to hurry out of work unnoticed. But this time, I spoke up.

"Yes," I said loudly. "It's me in the photo."

A couple of writers whispered to each other; others were stunned silent. My heart pounded against my rib cage as I looked around the room. I inched toward the doorway.

"And I'm in love with Scarlett Daniels."

Gasps circled the news office as women covered their open mouths with dainty, manicured hands. Most of the men just sort of raised their eyebrows. With that bold declaration, my sweaty palm turned the brass doorknob in front of me and I strutted out with my head held high, a coy smile dancing across my lips. I thought I heard Giselle call my name, but I was walking too quickly to turn back.

Chapter 49

The high lasted for twenty blocks. I was all smiles as I made my way home. The rain stopped for a moment and I gazed up at the misty sky, wondering if Scarlett was looking at the same sherbet mass that I was. Baby blues and soft pinks whirled around behind a cloudy curtain.

Scarlett. I needed to find her. As I raced through my apartment's entrance, I knew that I had been wrong to get angry. This was her way—her grand gesture. I stepped into the shower minutes later and let hot water run over my tense shoulders, thinking of what I would say to Scarlett as I inhaled the steam. Different ideas tangoed through my head until my fingers started to prune.

I toweled off and slipped into a turquoise swing dress. It had been a while since I'd chosen something so bright. I rolled a pair of nude stockings over my knees and waited for my hair to dry. Then I brushed out each strand and secured a tight twist at the nape of my neck.

My makeup arsenal was sparse and underused. Nonetheless, I managed to apply liner and black mascara that made my eyes sparkle. I smiled and swirled a poppy blush over my cheeks. Then I selected a pair of clip-on pearl earrings and their matching necklace. It hung just above my collarbone, right beside a light brown beauty mark I'd hated as a girl. For some reason, it didn't bother me anymore.

I phoned the local cab company and stepped into a pair of black pumps I hadn't worn since 1925. A while later, I grabbed my herringbone trench coat and locked the door behind me. My keys rattled around my evening clutch as I pranced down the stairs. After months of despondency, I had come back to life.

＊

THE taxi ride to New York City dragged on like dripping molasses. I shifted excitedly in my seat every time we passed another avenue. Robbie had told me which hotel Scarlett was staying at. When we finally pulled up in front of the Waldorf Astoria, I nearly jumped out of the cab.

I kept a low profile as I walked through the ornate lobby. Crystal chandeliers hung from vaulted ceilings and a pianist played soft classical music. The scent of expensive perfume and cigars emanated through the room. My heels wobbled under the weight of my anticipation as I reached the elevator towers.

I stepped inside and took another look around the lobby. Wealthy patrons sipped their scotches and bourbons, engaged in light business chatter. Ladies in flouncy dresses trailed reluctantly behind their husbands, rolling their smoky eyes. My lungs tightened as the elevator doors closed and I left the ritzy reception area behind.

When they reopened, I was standing on the seventeenth floor. I adjusted my pearl necklace and walked slowly to room 1795. Somewhere during the elevator ride, my overactive nerves had been replaced with a welcome sense of calm. I was ready to see her.

I paused outside Scarlett's room, allowing myself one last deep breath. After a few quiet knocks, I heard her padded footsteps on the other side of the hotel door. It flung open moments later to reveal my truest love, standing sweetly in a pair of striped pink pajamas. As I threw myself into her warm embrace, Scarlett's familiar touch and disarming affection enveloped me all at once.

She hugged me tightly as the door closed softly behind us. Our bodies pressed together and I inhaled her signature scent, the one that used to intoxicate me beyond belief. Over the years, the aroma had become pure comfort and ease.

Eventually, Scarlett pulled back to meet my eyes. I felt the inevitable quickening of my heart as we connected.

"I'm sorry it took me so long," she whispered.

After that, there were no words. And although mere weeks had passed since our last encounter, we shared a different sort of love that night. No coyness, no games. Only us.

※

I woke up to the sound of Scarlett humming. She was perched by the window, staring out at the New York skyline. The pale sunlight told me it was still morning. I smiled as she put her hand gracefully on the glass pane and traced the skyscrapers from left to right, pausing slightly at the Chrysler Building.

I closed my eyes and listened to her serene humming. I wanted to wake up to that calming sound every morning for the rest of my life.

When I stirred up again, she was back in bed, tucked cozily by my side. Her blond hair, still lustrous as ever, was shorter than it had been in Hong Kong. It curled subtly at the ends and framed her stunning face. As I began to visually trace her chiseled bone structure, she opened her eyes and beamed.

"Let's run away," she whispered.

I looked at her illuminated eyes—sparkling green, just like when we were young.

"Okay."

"I'm serious."

"I know." I inched closer to her.

"*Really?*" Scarlett asked in disbelief.

"We'll run away together to any place you'd like."

The corners of her mouth crept into a beautiful smile, and then she kissed me deeply. I was convinced that we could be happy anywhere, so long as we were together. We both sighed as I pulled her into another long embrace. It was a moment of pure, untainted bliss.

Chapter 50

Bermuda, March 1950

The island breeze blew through my hair as I waded into the cerulean shallows. Hot sand beneath my feet turned into smooth, algae-covered rocks and tiny white seashells. I smelled nothing but salty air and the fresh fruit hanging from the abundant trees above. I loved the carefree vibe of the beach, locals fishing on the north shore while vacationers sipped rum and sangria.

I looked at Scarlett, floating atop the quiet waves as sun tanned her alabaster skin. She was wearing the striped bathing costume we'd found in our hotel gift shop. It hugged her petite curves as her thin frame bobbed gently up and down in the turquoise ocean. Her large oval sunglasses and perfect blond hair made me laugh. Scarlett couldn't pull off incognito to save her life.

We retreated to the sandy bank once the tide rose. Our villa was near the south shore, conveniently isolated from other tourists. We had arrived the week prior after finally choosing Bermuda from a long list of exotic locales. We were city lovers at heart, but the tropical setting agreed with both of us.

In the mornings, we sipped local coffee and read on the patio. Then we headed to the beach and lay under the sun until one of us—usually me—became restless. Then it was fresh fish for lunch in a casual restaurant before returning to the beach. Scarlett took some convincing to go into the water at first. But now here we were, just a few days later, immersed in the sea until the tide forced us out.

The evenings were magic. When the island sun set into the broad stretch of lapis ocean outside our villa, the purple sky lit up fiery orange just for a moment before the sun disappeared. Twilight in Bermuda was something out of a dream as well. Moonlight shone onto the black waves as wooden torches illuminated the empty beach. The sky had more stars than either of us had ever seen. There was nothing more radiant and possessing.

~※~

WE returned to the villa early for an alfresco dinner. Scarlett bought fresh fillets from the outdoor market and I scoured the vegetable garden near our holiday home. She told me that she was feeling especially tired, so I urged her to take a nap while I cooked.

I fetched seasonings from the pantry as the skillet warmed— a sprinkle of chives, two dashes of sea salt, and a generous pat of butter. I delighted in the sizzling sound the ingredients made as they melted in the hot pan. I lightly seared each fillet until golden brown streaks appeared. Then I plated the fish over a bed of mixed greens and caramelized onions.

Scarlett was fast asleep when I tiptoed into our airy bedroom. Sun shone through the sheer peach curtains, and specks of light peeked out between the thick plantation shutters. I could hear the regular afternoon commotion as local children played games outside, but Scarlett didn't seem to mind. She was sleeping more soundly than I'd ever seen her do.

Her body took up only a small fraction of our roomy mattress. An open suitcase sat at the foot of the bed, summery clothes hanging out of it. I walked over to straighten up, careful not to wake Scarlett. As I lifted her luggage flap, a small bottle fell out the suitcase and rolled under our bed. I bent over to pick it up, glancing at Scarlett before kneeling down quietly.

I reached far underneath the bed frame and felt around aimlessly for a few moments before finally making contact. The clear glass bottle was covered in dust by the time I grabbed it. I wiped off the tiny label and squinted to read its impossibly small lettering. It was a prescription:

Scarlett M. Daniels—Take two tablets per day or as needed for pain.

Chapter 51

My first instinct was to toss the pills back into her suitcase and leave the room. But I continued to stare at the bottle, clenching it until my knuckles turned white. I turned it over as I wondered what the pills might be for. When I opened her suitcase to put them back, a tiny pink paper caught my attention. I plucked it up and read the messy pencil script:

> As discussed, the cancer has already spread rapidly. We've covered the lack of treatment options, so I'm prescribing you medication for pain management. Take it as needed, per bottle directions. Do not exceed six tablets in one day.

When Scarlett started to stir, I panicked and stuck the note and pills into my dress pocket before hurrying back into the kitchen.

I put our dinner back into the oven and waited patiently for her to come out. She never did. An hour passed by while I sat at our glass dining table, shifting uncomfortably in the wooden chair. I played with my apron strings as the fish lost its fresh taste and the greens wilted.

I reached into my pocket hesitantly and fingered the sturdy lid of the bottle. My heart raced as I turned it slowly around. I wondered how many times Scarlett had opened it. I shook my head and pulled the bottle back out. The tiny lettering stared at me menacingly until I set it down on the glass table. I rested my face in my open palms, hoping that Scarlett would emerge before sundown.

Another hour, and still nothing. I felt guilty when I realized that the cancer was probably draining her energy. It was good for her to sleep. I wrapped up our meal and stuck it in the fridge; all the worrying had spoiled my appetite. Then I sat on the patio to take in Bermuda's inimitable sunset.

Spidery vines and island flowers covered the deck. The dim, humid air encased me as I sat underneath a pretty ivy arch. I sank deeper into my wicker chair as ginger swirls tangled with rich amethyst blocks of sky. In that moment, the sunset relaxed me more than anything else could.

I remained seated long after the sun disappeared. My sleeveless dress left my exposed shoulders chilled, but I was lost in something else. I couldn't stop thinking about the medicine and Scarlett's diagnosis. Normally, I would have rushed to her side and asked her what was going on. But the tiny piece of pink paper made her condition perfectly clear: cancer.

I was sad of course. But more than anything, I was stunned. And as time passed, that shock turned into confusion. *When did she find out about this?* It felt like the biggest secret of all had been right under my nose all along, hidden in an expensive suitcase.

As the rest of the town slept peacefully, I became more

restless. My racing thoughts and the cool evening breeze kept me awake. I stood up to fetch a sweater, but paced around the patio instead. As it got darker, the worst thought of all hit me. Everything that Scarlett had said and done recently was out of fear. *It was the cancer.* She hadn't made a grand gesture in Times Square. *She just didn't want to die alone.*

꠸

I woke up to the sound of eastern bluebirds scurrying around on the ivy above me. They delicately perched atop the arch and sucked nectar from its tiny flowers. I realized my exhausting mental rant the night before had sent me to sleep before I could make it back inside. I shifted in the cushioned wicker chair and massaged my tight neck muscles.

The atmosphere was heavier and more humid than it had been the previous day. Morning dew clung to the courtyard's tropical plants as the scent of sweet blossoms filled the air. I stood up and felt tingles in my legs from sitting for so long. My hair was matted and sticky with sweat.

I walked inside for a morning shower, closing the patio door quietly behind me in case Scarlett was still resting. My heart stopped when I saw her sitting near the table, staring at the glass bottle of pills. She looked at me with empty eyes.

"Hi, Lia."

I nodded slowly, lost for words.

"I see you found these," she said, picking up the bottle and giving it a little shake. *"And my doctor's note."*

The sound of the pills clanking together made my ears hurt.

"While I was sleeping?"

I nodded again.

"I found out while I was in Hong Kong."

I stared at her, wondering what to say.

"It was after you left," she continued. "I started having odd symptoms on set. My dad took me to a well-known clinic on the other side of the city . . ."

I pictured Mac forcing Scarlett to go. She had always been resistant in that way.

"They tried so many things in such a short period of time. Different tests and treatments"—I sat down next to Scarlett as her voice broke—"Nothing worked."

I looked at her gaunt face and wondered why I hadn't noticed it before. To me, she looked as healthy and vibrant as ever. The more I stared, though, the more I noticed. Puffy bags under her tired eyes contradicted the hours of sleep she'd just gotten.

I knew that I should comfort her, but my skepticism from the night before still had control. "Why didn't you tell me?"

"I didn't know how," she whispered.

"You could have written me."

"After the way things ended in Hong Kong?"

"You should have been honest at the hotel in New York," I said curtly.

"Lead with *that* news? I wanted to win you back, not make you feel sorry for me—"

"Yeah? Well, your *grand* gesture seems a little less impressive now."

"How can you say that?"

"It's obvious that we wouldn't even be here if you—"

"Please, Lia," she interrupted. "I did the press conference because I realized what a mistake I'd made."

I stared into her green eyes, searching for the truth.

"You were always so sure of everything," she said, smiling. "And I . . . well, I wasn't. It took me this long to figure out that happiness has been here the whole time. I just needed to accept who I am . . . who *we* are."

I put my hand on hers and spoke again. "I'm proud of you for that. And announcing it to the world . . ."

"I know." She laughed. "We're public news."

"Regardless, we should get you to an American clinic—"

"I've already been to see the best doctor in New York, Lia. He says there's nothing they can do . . ."

My heart sank as I looked at her fragile expression. As much as I didn't want to believe it, I understood her tone.

"I'm sorry." She leaned closer.

I shook my head. "You don't have to be."

My cynicism dissolved as I realized that it was pointless to stay angry. Scarlett loved me like I loved her. No matter what happened, we always found a way back to each other.

Chapter 52

SCARLETT

I fade more every single day. It's a defeating process, this illness. It breaks your spirit as it sucks the life out of you. Sometimes I wonder if I should be trying harder. I did at first, visit after visit. But nothing worked. Every single doctor said the same exact thing: "There's nothing to be done." I wanted to be angry—to scream, cry, and yell. I wanted to, but I couldn't. The truth is, I don't fault them at all. This is beyond their control.

Most days, I just feel exhausted. I want to keep up with her, but I can't. It's frustrating, to say the least. But I'm too tired to get frustrated these days. So I just smile. It's so easy to smile when I'm around Lia.

I understand why she got upset. I didn't tell her, and then she found that stupid bottle in my suitcase. She has every right to be furious, but the anger didn't last. She's incredible, my Lia. As difficult as this is for me, I think it's even harder for her.

Chapter 53

LIA

The pills. There were so many pills. Blue gel, brown syrup, grainy beige, canary yellow. As it turned out, that clear glass bottle I found was just one of many. And she had to take them at specific times throughout the day, tying us to a rigid schedule of medicating and monitoring. Scarlett calmly explained that the pills weren't treating her cancer but rather the pain that came with it. She'd chosen the only option available, allowing the disease to intensify until it ended her.

We tried to enjoy the rest of our time on the island as much as possible. The moist air and healing sea were good for Scarlett. But there were also days when she couldn't get out of bed. Initially, I'd try to wake her and make her eat something. I took my job as her stand-in nurse very seriously. I'd deliver her two yellow capsules in the morning, and then I'd bring fruity yogurt or scrambled eggs and sausage. It was a futile effort; nausea usually got the best of her before she could get anything down. I quickly realized that I needed to let Scarlett rest whenever possible.

We made it to the beach on Friday afternoon. The whole

thing looked like a postcard. Olivewood trees, sapphire waves, not a soul in sight. I laid out towels and set up an umbrella to shield Scarlett from the harsh sun. Her striped bathing costume peeked out from underneath a white robe. She was covering up as much as she could, probably to hide her increasingly bony figure.

I tried desperately to convince her that there was still hope.

"Don't you want to go back home?"

She sighed and shook her head decisively.

"It might be smarter to return to the States. We could—"

"There's no cure, Lia." She spoke softly and looked at me through her dark sunglasses.

"I'm going to die."

There was an odd acceptance in her voice that made my stomach turn.

"I'm sorry it's all so sudden for you," she said. "I've had time to mourn this—"

"Well, I haven't," I said, tears pricking my eyes. "And I can't."

"I'm happy here. With *you*. I know it's not ideal, but we can spend the rest of—"

"Please don't," I whispered.

Her face fell. "Lia. You don't have to go through this, you know. I would understand if this is too hard."

"Don't be cruel," I said. "Of course I'm going to stay with you. I just wish you would fight this—"

"I don't want to fight this," she said defensively. "It's a futile effort. There's *nothing* I can do."

"I just don't understand. We're finally together after decades, and ..."

"I know, my love. It's not fair."

"It's not."

She put her hand over mine. "This is going to get very bad *very* quickly. I want you to remember the girl I used to be."

"I think pretty highly of the woman you've become." I smiled.

"But I—"

"You don't get it, Scarlett. I love all of you. Every. Single. Piece. You're more beautiful now than the first day I met you."

A shy smile crept across her pink lips. I rolled over and curled up next to her, warmed by the golden sand beneath our towels. I took her face in my hands and kissed her slowly.

"You're so much more than I deserve," she whispered.

As I ran my hand through her thinning blond hair, I knew she was completely wrong. We deserved each other more than anything in the world.

Chapter 54

The weeks passed much quicker than I hoped they would. It was officially May now, although Bermuda's weather made it feel like summer year-round. Scarlett's unwavering positivity tested my occasional pessimism. I tried to be strong for her, but most challenging moments ended in defeat.

We both knew that she was fading at a quicker rate each day. Despite the pain pills, cancer was winning. We could no longer leave the villa or make it to the beach. I went out to buy food every couple of days, while Scarlett slept or read in bed.

Sometimes I'd make an excuse to leave so I could cry without her knowing. I saw how hard she was fighting every single day, just for another moment together. But her fake smile rarely fooled me anymore.

It broke my heart to see her in so much pain. There were days I wished I wasn't with her, simply so she could let go in peace. Scarlett would probably be gone by now if she was alone. It had gotten to the point where she was just plain *existing*. And for what?

One particularly warm evening, I persuaded her to sit outside on the patio with me. I lit candles and set them around the courtyard so that some of the greenest plants were illuminated.

The flowers were in full bloom and the whole area smelled like sweet nectar. I made Scarlett close her eyes as I helped her walk out. Her big smile when she opened them was validation enough for my efforts.

After a light dinner, we moved to a wooden bench on the opposite side of the villa. Scarlett leaned her head on my shoulder as we both stared at the stars. I felt her faint breath quicken as her weak grip tightened around my hand. The fragile sound of her stillness felt entirely foreign.

I kissed her cheek softly and felt her heartbeat accelerate. What used to be a thrilling sensation now only seemed to worry me.

"Are you okay?"

She tilted her head and looked at me sweetly. "Try not to worry about me."

"That's impossible," I whispered.

I felt her smile as she leaned her soft head on my shoulder. "Try, Lia."

"I'll always worry about you."

"I don't want you to be miserable and lonely. I want you to live like we're still in love."

"You are the *solitary* love of my life, Scarlett. That won't change once . . ." I couldn't finish my sentence.

"Once I'm gone," she said, closing her eyes tightly.

We both knew what was going to happen, but I hated the sound of it. Most days, I pushed that awful thought to the furthest corners of my brain. But when she verbalized it like this, the truth came reeling forward, threatening my composed facade.

"We did it, didn't we?"

I looked at her face, barely visible in the dim light. "Did what?"

"Gave it our best shot," she whispered.

I saw watery tears in her eyes, reflecting the radiant stars above us. The whole thing was almost too symbolic. I used to love those stars . . . I worshipped them because they reminded me of us. But in that moment, I hated them with every beat of my heart.

"My love," she said as if she knew exactly what I was thinking. "Don't be angry."

I turned my head and looked at the outline of her face.

"It's not anyone's fault," she said. "Stars are just stars."

I didn't reply.

"Stars are just stars," she whispered again.

Chapter 55

East China Sea, September 1953

Massive waves crash against the side of our ship as I make my way starboard. All I can see are stretches of misty ocean in every direction. My eyes haven't fully adjusted to the salty air, but I'm glad that I agreed to come. After a lot of planning, I'm on a sailing trip with my father, Robbie, and Mac.

We're an unlikely bunch, but we get along surprisingly well together. This trip is exactly what I needed after Scarlett's passing. Mac joined us in Bermuda during the very end, and then we had a small ceremony back in London. It was short and sweet, just like she would have wanted.

Mac encouraged me to travel before going back to work, but I declined. Still, he insisted that I try my hand at backpacking or sailing. *Somethin' to take the edge off,* as he put it. When he wouldn't let up, I agreed to a postponed voyage. After a couple of years passed, I knew I was finally ready to move on. Scarlett loved the sea, so I agreed to a three-week sailing trip as long as my dad and Robbie could join us.

Tonight, after a late meal, we all play cards, just like Mac used to do with his sailing buddies. It's a nice distraction from my usual routine of dinner and report editing. I'm not feeling great, so I retire early to my tiny sleeping quarters in the middle of the ship.

I toss and turn in my bunk before I realize that I'm not going to fall asleep tonight. Mac warned us that the waves would be rockier for the next few days. Midnight strikes, and I know that it's time to do something I've avoided for a while.

I open my cabin door and feel an immediate rush of frigid wind. After making sure I'm absolutely alone, I sneak out onto the main deck. My wild hair blows all over my face before I quickly tuck it behind my ears. It's an odd feeling to be alone on the deck, especially at night. My pajamas and boots are no match for this blustery weather.

I open the wooden box I'm holding and feel tears roll down my chilled cheeks. I can barely see the vial of gray dust in this dim evening light. I clutch it tightly in my left hand.

We're sitting on the patio one last time, our final day together.

"Will you do something for me?"

I look at her ghost-like face and nod.

"My ashes," she whispers.

I immediately wish that I was the sick one . . . that I would die and Scarlett would live. It's not selfless, but actually quite selfish. Of course I don't want her to suffer from this pain any longer, but it's more than that. I don't want to be the person who gets to live, who has to live. I can't bury her body and move on without her. I don't know if I'm strong enough.

"I want to be sprinkled into the sea." Scarlett's eyes light up for the first time in weeks.

"The sea?"

"Yes, Lia. I loved it there when I was a girl . . ."

She proceeds to tell me all about Mac and their adventures together, as if I've never met him. As if he's not waiting for us inside the villa, making coffee. Her memory hasn't been sharp for days. I'm not sure if it's the medicine, the sickness, or both. She's not herself anymore.

Briny seawater sprays my face as I lose my balance. I grab onto the side of the ship and try not to fall. We're sailing so quickly through the darkness, it's impossible to catch my breath. All I want is to crawl back into bed and pretend this isn't happening. But her voice reminds me what I have to do. *I want to be sprinkled into the sea.*

I uncork the vial and watch Scarlett's ashes descend softly into the water below. My eyes tear up as they fall like pixie dust. I'm weeping now, choking back sobs as my salty tears mix with the murky ocean waves.

The current picks up as I continue to pour Scarlett out. Suddenly, a gust of marine wind steals the glass vial from my hand. I cry out as it goes crashing toward the black water's depth. But a final clump of ashes escapes, caught in the unavoidable breeze of this September night, and I watch in awe as they dance in the wind, soaring up and down and up again. The tiny flecks are paralleling our ship now, picking up speed as we cut through the water. My strained eyes are glued to Scarlett's ashes.

The last pieces I can see have almost vanished. Another gust whisks them up before they disappear permanently into the obscure air. And then she's gone. Now I can't hold on to anything but intangible memories of her.

I stare into the dark expanse and let the mind-numbing cold wash over me. Everything is a blur as I blink back the unrelenting tears. The air is still again; the only sound I hear is the constant roar of ocean waves. I wipe my eyes and soften slightly when I realize what I'm staring at. It's the shining night sky we used to find irresistible, dotted with shimmering stars big and small.

Despite everything that's happened, I refuse to hate the stars. Scarlett said that *stars are just stars*, but I still think they're something more. Maybe they have nothing to do with fate or destiny, but they do remind me of us. Because people are like stars, if you really think about it. Some of us live in constellations, forever connected by something that once was. But others spark like shooting stars, brilliantly lighting up this world before moving on to the next.

END

About the Author

DANIELLE M. WONG is an emerging author living in San Francisco. Writer by day and reader by night, she loves creating and consuming all forms of media. Beyond her love of writing, Danielle is a passionate traveler and photographer. She was fortunate enough to tag along on her father's business trips during childhood, and has explored more than 25 different countries. Seeing so much of the world at a young age shaped her unique perspective on life.

Her writing has been published on several websites, including *The Huffington Post, USA Today,* and *Her Campus.* She has a short story published in *Be The Star You Are For Teens,* and is currently working on her next novel.

SELECTED TITLES FROM SHE WRITES PRESS

She Writes Press is an independent publishing company
founded to serve women writers everywhere.
Visit us at www.shewritespress.com.

The Doctor and the Stork: A Memoir of Modern Medical Babymaking by
K.K. Goldberg. $16.95, 978-1-63152-830-9. A mother's compelling
story of her post-IVF, high-risk pregnancy with twins—the very
definition of a modern medical babymaking experience.

Expecting Sunshine: A Journey of Grief, Healing, and Pregnancy after Loss
by Alexis Marie Chute. $16.95, 978-1-63152-174-4. A mother's in-
spiring story of surviving pregnancy following the death of one of
her children at birth.

A Leg to Stand On: An Amputee's Walk into Motherhood by Colleen Hag-
gerty. $16.95, 978-1-63152-923-8. Haggerty's candid story of how
she overcame the pain of losing a leg at seventeen—and of terminat-
ing two pregnancies as a young woman—and went on to become a
mother, despite her fears.

Breathe: A Memoir of Motherhood, Grief, and Family Conflict by Kelly
Kittel. $16.95, 978-1-938314-78-0. A mother's heartbreaking account
of losing two sons in the span of nine months—and learning, despite
all the obstacles in her way, to find joy in life again.

Make a Wish for Me: A Mother's Memoir by LeeAndra Chergey. $16.95,
978-1-63152-828-6. A life-changing diagnosis teaches a family that
where's there is love there is hope—and that being "normal" is not
nearly as important as providing your child with a life full of joy,
love, and acceptance.

Three Minus One: Parents' Stories of Love & Loss edited by Sean Hanish
and Brooke Warner. $17.95, 978-1-938314-80-3. A collection of sto-
ries and artwork by parents who have suffered child loss that offers
insight into this unique and devastating experience.